DARK MURAL

Nicole Tang Noonan Mystery #1

By Rick Homan

D1607669

First published 2018
Copyright 2018 by Rick Homan
www.RickHoman.com

Acknowledgements

I am grateful to my Sisters in Crime (and brothers); my fellow writers and the librarians at the Mechanics' Institute Library in San Francisco; and most of all to my wife, Ann.

Rick Homan

Chapter 1

As I sat at an umbrella table in front of Emma's Deli in Blanton, Ohio, a man walking up the street stopped a few yards away and stared at me.

It wasn't the five-second stare. Everyone I met in Ohio needed five seconds to stare when they laid eyes on me for the first time. It took them that long to understand they were meeting an Asian woman with freckles. The only exceptions to this rule were people who had seen my name, Nicole Tang Noonan, on my resume. They needed only three seconds.

I couldn't be sure of the expression on his face because he was silhouetted against a bright sky, but I had the feeling his upper lip was raised in disgust. He wore work boots, jeans, a t-shirt, and a cap with a logo I didn't recognize.

The sight of him made my skin crawl.

When Abbie came out of the deli and sat on the other side of the table, he shook his head and walked on by.

I looked to Abbie for an explanation. "What's his problem?"

"Trust me: You don't want to know."

Abbie Krauss, assistant professor of economics, was my new best friend. We both lived in the section of on-campus housing devoted to single faculty: a series of wooden sheds with no porches and no landscaping, set in straight lines on either side of a gravel road. They looked like the kind of unit provided as disaster relief for evacuees after a flood or hurricane. We called them Rabbit Hutches.

"I guess people around here aren't used to seeing Asians unless they're running a restaurant," I said. The family, who operated the Golden Palace two blocks away, were the only Asians I had seen outside of Columbus. This was mind-boggling for me since I was from San Francisco where a third of the people are Asian.

Abbie shook her head. "Not everyone around here is like that. His name is Huey Littleton. He's part of a big, extended family—lots of cousins—and most of them have never been more than fifty miles from home. They've been here quite a few generations, so they seem to think the entire county should be only for people like them."

"White people?"

Abbie nodded. "Preferably relatives."

"So what am I supposed to do? Bow and step aside when he passes by?"

"I know it's insulting, but it's the way things are here, and in a way it works. For instance, over on Maple Street, there are two bars, Buddy's and Marten's Tavern. Buddy's is for locals like Huey. Anyone from the college would take their life in their hands if they went there on a Saturday night. Marten's is where students can go and nobody bothers them."

"Charming," I said. "Be sure to tell me if there's anything else I can do to avoid frightening the horses."

"So what did you want to talk about?" asked Abbie.

"My first week of classes is not exactly taking flight."

"Welcome to the club."

"I've heard there's a mural in the chapel that dates from the time of the Civil War."

"Yes, there is."

"So you've seen it?" I asked. "What's it like?"

"It depicts the group led by Felix Fuchs who came here from Germany and established the religious commune, which eventually became Fuchs College."

"How can I get in to take a look at it?"

"Drop by Facilities Management and sign out a key. What

are you thinking?"

"If the mural is any good, I'd like to meet my art history class in the chapel. I think my students would be more interested in learning about the history of someone else's art if they first looked at some art that is part of their own college's history."

"Sounds like a good idea," said Abbie. "Let me know how it goes. There's another thing you might do. Have you met Jacob Schumacher?"

The name did not ring a bell. I shook my head.

"He's the chairman of the history department. He'll be glad to hear that you're taking an interest in the mural or anything to do with the history of the place. One of his ancestors was part of that original group who came here from Germany. It's a good idea to have him on your side."

Key in hand, I walked down College Avenue to the chapel. It was a plain, square building about thirty-five feet on each side with an entry hall on the west. No effort had been made to create an impression on the visitor; no materials had been squandered. It had no steeple. What charm it had, it achieved through proportion. In this it reminded me of the Shaker furniture I had seen in museums. The German immigrants who settled this land were not Shakers, but they lived in similar circumstances and apparently made what they needed in the same spirit. They took pleasure in simplicity.

The eastern side of the building had windows all the way across to provide ample morning light. The north side had no windows, and that was where the mural had been painted. I couldn't make out any detail as I peered in, but I could tell it covered the entire wall and included several vignettes.

I let myself in, walked to the center of the large room, took in the mural, and was struck by its power. It was what we used to call folk art. This artist may have been untrained but was not unpracticed. Most important, the work was free of pretension. He or she had not felt any need to emulate the

7

styles of great artists or strive for some conventional notion of beauty. Instead, he had developed his own vocabulary and used it to communicate what was important to him.

The mural contained several scenes and dozens of figures—men, women, and children—perhaps more than a hundred. They filled the wall, which was more than thirty feet wide and almost as high, plus a triangular space above, reaching to the roofline. The primary colors looked washed out, either because time had faded them or because the mural needed cleaning. Behind all the other images was a single tree with its roots in the ground near the floor and its crown filling the space near the ceiling. It was so faint that it appeared as if through fog, and everything else shone in front of it.

I began to wonder what I had gotten myself into. I had expected to find a simple landscape with some cows on the hillsides and a few houses. This mural was complex and detailed. Rather than viewing one scene from a single perspective, it included multiple scenes, each in its own perspective, as if the artist wanted to show things happening simultaneously. It was going to take me a while to understand the work before I could sort out what I would present to my students.

Monday morning was chilly, a reminder that my first Ohio winter was coming. I set out with a spring in my step to walk to the chapel, eager to meet my students and see how they would respond to a real work of art.

I don't know what made me glance at my little yellow car as I left my Rabbit Hutch, but, when I did, I saw black spray paint on the hood. The crude, slashing lines spelled, "JAP OUT." Frozen in my tracks, I guessed that, if "JAP" was a reference to Asians in general, then I was looking at a racist slur, and it was aimed at me. My heart started thumping.

I looked up and down Montgomery Avenue to see if anyone else was around or if any of my neighbors was looking out a window. I suppose I wanted witnesses, though I was also looking for anyone with a can of spray paint in his hand. I saw no one.

I pulled out my phone to call campus security and noticed I had about ten minutes until it was time to meet my students. Not wanting to be late for my own class, I started jogging toward the chapel.

Chapter 2

No one was waiting when I got to the chapel, so I unlocked the door and phoned security. As I recited the few facts I had to the dispatcher, my students came walking up College Avenue, and I waved them inside. The dispatcher promised to send a car, we hung up, and I took a moment to calm the rage building inside me and focus on art history before going in.

With the students sitting in a semicircle, facing the mural, I was about to speak when I heard voices from the front door.

"I told you we'd be late," said Kate Conrad, an especially enthusiastic student of art history, today wearing a sequined t-shirt, jeans, and ballet flats with a satin varsity-style jacket. Devon Manus, who usually seemed more interested in Kate than she was in him, followed her. He looked as if he had gotten out of bed just in time to throw on a t-shirt, jeans, sneakers and a bomber jacket.

After they found chairs, I said, "Look at the mural."

Most of the students glanced at the wall for a few seconds, then looked back at me. Kate kept her eyes on the mural, moving them from side to side and top to bottom.

"What did you see?" I asked.

Ursula Wilmot scowled. As usual, she was dressed as if on her way to an office job and had her ring binder open on her lap, ready to take notes.

Byron Hawley, dressed in a t-shirt, jeans, and sneakers, all smeared with many colors of paint, so everyone would know he was an artist, said, "Poor use of perspective. Little sense of anatomy. Limited color palette."

Kate said, "The life of a community."

Looking around the room, I asked, "What goes on in this community?"

This got some of them squirming in their seats. Ursula Wilmot now had both hands wrapped around her ballpoint pen as if she were about to snap it in two.

Kate spoke up. "Work. Worship. Life and Death."

"Let's take another look," I said.

They all looked at the mural, and their eyes were busy.

"Keep looking," I said, as I walked around them and went to where I had left my backpack and shopping bag on a chair by the lectern. I tore two sheets for each of them off a pad of newsprint. I also gave each of them a crayon. "Maybe we should take some notes."

Most of them put their books and backpacks in their laps and started making tiny marks on the newsprint. Kate got an extra chair on which to rest her feet and started drawing. Devon sat an arm's length away from her, glancing first at the mural, then at Kate's drawing, and then doodling on his own sheet.

"Are these going to be graded?" asked Ursula. Her sheet of newsprint was still blank.

"If anyone asks me that again, I will grade them," I replied.

Everyone got to work.

I walked around the room, sneaking peeks at their drawings just to make sure they were giving it the old college try. Some of the students were making clusters of tiny figures, separated by lots of open space. Byron Hawley had produced an accurate sketch of the lower half of the mural and was adding his own details and shading. Devon's page was a collection of starts and stops: stick figures without arms, a tree with only half its crown.

Kate's page was a wild collection of stick figures with

punctuation marks, circles, arrows, and dotted lines that seemed to suggest relationships. She was the only one to represent all parts of the mural: the scenes of work across the bottom of the wall, the scenes of worship across the upper part, and the crown of the tree reaching to the roofline. It looked like she was making connections between images and interpreting the overall layout.

In other words, she was doing what I'd done yesterday afternoon when I spent a couple of hours with the mural. How does a student in a beginner's art history course understand a work of art on a level usually achieved by graduate students? I started getting excited, thinking about how much Kate might accomplish this semester.

After a while I stood before them again and asked, "What goes on in this community?"

This time the answers came quickly. They were looking at their drawings as they called them out. "Farming . . . I think they're harvesting wheat . . . Picking fruit . . . Cooking . . . Must have been Thanksgiving dinner. There are five women in the kitchen . . . I counted six . . . Is that one guy giving a sermon? . . . Building something . . . I don't know what those people in the middle are doing . . . I think that group of people on the right are singing in a choir . . . What are those little things at the top? . . . It's hard to see up there."

Our fifty-minute period was almost done. "I think we know a lot more about this mural than we did when we walked in this morning. Do you think we've seen all there is to see?"

Kate laughed and said, "I think there might be a few things we haven't picked up yet."

"My point here is that we look at something, and think we've seen it, but when we start looking for things, we understand that there's a lot more to see."

I was starting to sound like Obi Wan Kenobi, so I decided to wrap it up. "Keep your drawings handy. We'll refer to them again. I'll see you on Wednesday."

Someone called out, "Are we meeting here again?"

"No. In the classroom."

They packed up and started leaving. Kate approached me and said, "I've been at this school three years, and I've never been in here and seen this mural. It's really interesting."

"I'm glad you think so."

"If we're not going to meet in here again, is there some way I could come in and look at it some more?"

These were words every teacher wants to hear. "I might come in Thursday afternoon to study it," I said. "You're welcome to join me."

"Thanks, I will," she said. With that, she turned and headed for the door.

Devon also stopped to talk to me. "Great class, Dr. Noonan. I really learned a lot."

From the door Kate made a loud kissing sound, laughed, and walked out. I was surprised to see Devon look embarrassed at having his tactic exposed.

"Thank you, Devon," I said. "I'm glad you learned a lot. I'll see you on Wednesday."

He trotted off toward the door like a golden retriever with a tennis ball.

I dropped my backpack and shopping bag in my office and walked over to the snack bar in the Student Services Center, which looked out on a lawn that was bounded by the library and the Old Classroom Building. Both of those buildings dated from the 1920s and had been designed in the collegiate gothic style. The pointed arches and carved ornaments gave the impression of a medieval European town. By contrast the Student Services Center, which had been built in the 1970s, had the feeling of a shopping mall.

After eating most of my yogurt and banana, I called campus security. The woman I had spoken with was no longer answering the phone, so I had to give my name and explain why I had called earlier.

I heard a keyboard rattling before the officer said, "Yes, I have the incident report in front of me. Patrol was dispatched at 10:03. The officer reported the words, 'JAP OUT,' spray-painted on the hood of a yellow Toyota Tercel. A photograph is attached to the report. What is your question?"

"I'm new to this campus, so I'm wondering what security does in a situation like this."

"In any instance of vandalism, we increase patrols in the area. We'll also search our database for similar recent reports to see if there's a pattern."

"I see. Have there been other instances of messages like this spray-painted anywhere on campus?"

"I don't have that information in front of me. If you like, Dr. Noonan, I can attach a note to this report and have someone give you a call when that's available."

I agreed to that suggestion, thanked him, and hung up. I was a little surprised he didn't address the possibility that this was a hate crime. I needed to think about whether to pursue that angle on top of trying to get three courses on track, learn my way around a new school, and get around to shopping for some winter clothing. I decided for the moment to wait and see what campus security would come up with, but my mind was in such a state that further routine work was out of the question. I packed up and headed back to my Rabbit Hutch. It was time to find out who spray-painted my car.

Chapter 3

After a quick change from classroom biz-casual into a tank-top and knit pants with a flannel over shirt, I walked up Montgomery Avenue to the next Rabbit Hutch and knocked on the door. No one answered. The same happened at the next Rabbit Hutch and the one after that.

I turned up Ohio Avenue, which was lined on both sides with duplexes probably built around 1960. These were real houses, with peaked roofs, built of brick. I'd heard these went to couples with or without kids and sometimes to single faculty after they'd been on campus a few years.

After knocking on a few doors I found someone at home, introduced myself, waited for the five-second stare, told her what had happened to my car, and asked if she'd seen anyone who didn't live in the neighborhood passing by last evening or had heard anyone prowling around during the night. She said she hadn't, expressed disgust at what had been done to my car, and offered to help in any way she could.

I had the same conversation three more times as I worked my way up one side of Ohio Avenue and down the other, but my luck changed when I came to the next-to-the-last duplex, and the door was answered by an African-American man in his thirties. His black loafers were gleaming, his slacks had a knife-edge crease, and he wore a purple sweater that complemented his dark skin. He was only a few inches taller than me and neither heavy nor thin. He was compact, well-proportioned.

"Hi," I said, extending my hand. "Nicole Noonan. I'm

new here. I live right around the corner."

His stare took only two seconds. He took my hand, and said, "Lionel Bell. Welcome to the campus." His smile was warm and wide. "What department are you in?"

"Art. I'm the art historian. You?"

"French. Has your semester started off well?"

"It was going pretty well until I walked outside this morning and saw that someone had spray-painted the hood of my car."

"What?"

"I don't suppose you saw or heard anyone around here last night who shouldn't have been here."

He shook his head. "Do you think it happened here on campus?"

"It must have because it wasn't that way when I drove back from my errands on Saturday and parked next to my Rabbit Hutch."

"I'm so sorry to hear this." He stepped back from the doorway, and said, "Would you like to come inside and tell me about it?"

He didn't have to ask twice.

While he went to get me a glass of water, I took in the solid walls with wood moldings and felt the hardwood floor under my feet. His living room was furnished with a pleasant mix of personal effects and practical items. He had a fine oak armchair of the kind that was standard office furniture in the mid-twentieth century and a loveseat that might have been a family heirloom reupholstered. Other than that, the side tables, storage cubes, and area rug all looked like Ikea furniture, though of higher quality than the Ikea porch furniture I had purchased for my Rabbit Hutch.

Once I was on the loveseat with a glass of water, and he was seated in the chair across from me, he said, "I've never heard of this kind of vandalism on campus, and I've been here three years. I don't suppose that's any consolation."

"It may not be a simple matter of vandalism. Whoever did

it used the spray paint to write 'JAP OUT' on my hood."

That seemed to take his breath away for a moment. He shook his head and said, "I am so sorry to hear this has happened to you, especially when you've just arrived on campus. For what it's worth, I have not experienced any racial harassment here. It can get a little tense when I go into Blanton, but mostly it's live and let live."

"What really ticks me off is that my mother's family is Chinese, not Japanese."

He did his best to stifle a smile, but it grew and became a chuckle. "Excuse me. It's really not funny, but I was thinking how disappointing it is when racist vandals don't do their research."

That was funny, and we shared a good laugh. I got up to leave.

He had such a quiet way of listening, I felt free to bring up the next problem I had to face. "Do you know anything about getting spray paint off a car?"

"I'm afraid not," he said as we walked to the door. "If you end up having to take it to Chillicothe and leave it for the day, I'll be happy to drive over with you and give you a ride back to campus. And if there's anything else I can do to help you get settled . . ."

Smooth move. I appreciated that. "Actually, there is something. I've been buying my groceries at the market in Blanton, and they don't seem to have some things I'm looking for. I wonder if you might know the closest place to shop for some good cheeses. I'd love to get some genuine Roquefort. I'd also like to pick up some interesting sausages and pates, and I haven't found any place with a good wine selection."

Usually I don't make up things like this off the top of my head in the middle of a conversation, but he had given me a good opening, and I hated to waste it.

He smiled. "You won't find any of that this side of Columbus."

"Well, Columbus it is then. I've been meaning to go there

anyway and visit the Museum of Art."

"It's worth a visit. There are some significant pieces."

"I'm glad to hear that. If you recall the names of any good shops, would you email them to me? I'm in the campus directory."

I held my breath as I waited to see if he would take the bait.

Lionel pursed his lips before saying, "If you're free this Saturday, we could go up together and visit the museum. I'd be happy to take you around to some of my favorite shops afterward."

It is critical at moments like this to appear neither too surprised nor too delighted. "It's very generous of you to give up your Saturday for me."

"Not at all. I make the trip most weekends."

He offered to pick me up at ten o'clock so we could get there in time for lunch at the museum.

I walked to the next duplex, enjoying visions of an indoor picnic on Saturday evening: a loaf of bread, a jug of wine, a cheese board with interesting selections, and one lovely French professor beside me. Talking Lionel into a date was impulsive, but it felt right. Although I wasn't looking to start a relationship, there was no reason to swear off male companionship for the next year or two, and Lionel seemed like the perfect guy to provide it.

There was no one home on either side of the last duplex, but at the first Rabbit Hutch, around the corner on Montgomery Avenue, a woman about my age answered the door and introduced herself as a new hire in the English department. By the time I had explained my situation, I could tell by the look in her eyes she knew something.

"About two a. m., I heard tires on the gravel and an engine idling," she said. "My bedroom window faces the corner so anything going by at night wakes me up. I got freaked out when I heard footsteps, and got up to take a look. I heard a door slam. When I looked out, I saw a white pickup truck backing up Ohio Avenue."

My heart sped up and I started breathing as if I had reached my stride on my morning run. It was easy to visualize a man jumping out of a truck, trotting down the road, spray-painting my car, and high-tailing it back. He could have done it in less than a minute.

"Thanks," I said. "That's the first solid piece of information I've gotten. I don't suppose you noticed anything else about the truck. Was it new or old?"

She shook her head. "I don't know anything about trucks. Its headlights were off."

"That's interesting. Could you see the license plate?"

"No. Sorry."

I thanked her and said I would give this information to the campus police. She agreed to speak to them if they wanted to check.

I found no one else at home until I got to Abbie's Rabbit Hutch at the far end of Montgomery Avenue next to a grove of birches. I told her what had happened and what the new English professor on the corner had told me.

"One name comes to mind," she said, "but it doesn't make sense."

Chapter 4

Thinking back to my lunch with Abbie at the deli in Blanton, I knew who she had in mind. "Huey Littleton?"

She nodded.

"Does he drive a white pickup truck?"

She took a moment to think. "I can't remember."

"I thought you said there are rules around here so people don't run into people they don't like."

"That's why this doesn't make sense. If Huey came onto the campus to do this, he really crossed a line. I don't see why he would risk attracting attention here when he could have caught up with you somewhere else."

"Maybe the campus police will pay him some attention when I tell them about the white pickup truck."

Abbie looked skeptical. "I don't think their reach extends that far."

I was starting to feel angry again. "There has to be a way I can find out if Huey Littleton has a white truck and if he came by here last night."

"Whatever you do, don't go into Blanton looking for him. You do not want to cross paths with that man."

"Alright then, I'll keep calling campus security, and, if they won't call the sheriff I will."

She sighed. "I wish this hadn't happened right at the beginning of your first semester."

"It's not all bad," I replied. "Knocking on doors got me a date for Saturday."

"You're kidding! Who with?"

"Lionel Bell. Lives right around the corner."

"Ah, yes, Lionel. Well done. What's that saying about snatching victory from the jaws of defeat?"

"How about you?" I asked. "Do you have a boyfriend on campus?"

Abbie shook her head. "I'm not interested in guys."

"I'm sorry. I shouldn't have assumed."

She smiled. "Don't worry about it."

"Thanks for letting me know."

On Thursday afternoon, I got to the chapel a little before two thirty. The afternoon light was not strong enough for photos, so I got out the sketches and notes I had made on Sunday. While I was reviewing them, Kate Conrad came in, placed a chair for herself on the other side of the room, and started sketching and making notes.

The three scenes that made up the bottom row—working in the orchard, harvesting wheat, and working in the kitchen—formed a panorama of the community feeding itself. The artist put it at ground level, so the viewers could stand face-to-face with the workers—with themselves, really, thinking of the original viewers. In the central scene, only one face was visible. The farmer wearing green pants in the middle of the harvesting scene looked directly at the viewer. All the other workers turned away or had their faces partly obscured by the brim of a hat or a raised arm.

I heard footsteps coming from the entrance and looked over my shoulder in time to see a man coming through the door. As I got up and walked toward him, he said, "Don't let me disturb you. I saw the door open and thought I would come over and see who was here."

"Good afternoon," I said, "I'm Nicole Noonan."

"Jacob Schumacher," he said, extending his hand. No five-second stare from him.

This was the man Abbie had told me to have on my side, the chairman of the history department, whose ancestors were depicted in the mural I was studying, the man with whom I had made an appointment for next Tuesday. He was of medium height and a bit overweight. He wore his brown hair combed straight back from a hairline, which had receded very little though he must have been in his sixties. His mustache and goatee were trimmed so close that I wondered why he bothered letting them grow. He wore a blue blazer and gray slacks.

"I'm glad you dropped by," I said. "Maybe you can help me with some of the history behind this mural."

"I will if I can," he said. "I haven't been in here in years."

I filled him in on my observation that the face of only one of the workers was fully visible. As I spoke, I noticed that in the preaching scene, which was part of the upper row, only the preacher's face was completely visible. All the people in the congregation either had their backs to the viewer or had their faces partially blocked by someone next to them or by an open prayer book.

When I finished explaining, I turned to Jacob and saw him smiling and nodding. I knew the feeling. The pleasure that comes from a new idea is the chief reward for intellectual work.

I glanced back at the mural and saw something else. "The faces of the farmer and the preacher have a similar look. Both have long noses. I wonder why. Sometimes artists put their own faces into a crowd scene."

"And there's another one in the orchard," said Jacob. He walked to the wall and pointed to it. Again, the man with the long nose faced forward as in the preaching and harvesting scenes. "I think it's *Herr* Fuchs, the founder, Felix Fuchs. Have you seen photos of him? He had rather a long nose."

Kate, who had been walking back and forth, looking at the crown of the tree near the roofline, walked over to join us.

"This is my student, Kate Conrad," I said to Jacob. "Kate, this is Dr. Schumacher, chairman of the history department."

After they greeted one another Kate eyed the things I had taken out of my backpack. "Hey, Dr. Noonan," she said. "Are those your binoculars? Could I borrow them for a second?"

"Sure," I said. She went back to studying the details near the roofline.

Jacob smiled and nodded to show he was impressed with Kate's eagerness.

We continued our conversation as we walked outdoors "I'll let you return to your studies," said Jacob. "Thank you for sharing your work. I'll see you again when we meet next week."

"You're welcome," I said, "and thank you for helping me with the history of the commune. If I manage to publish an article about the mural, I'll acknowledge your contribution."

"That's not really necessary," he said, but I had the feeling he liked the idea.

After class on Friday morning, Kate stayed to talk to me, and of course Devon stayed to talk to her. "Great class, Dr. Noonan," he said. "Kate, I have to run, but can I pick you up about eight o'clock tonight?"

Kate turned to him with a scowl. "I don't know. I'll give you a call."

"All the usual crowd is going. We'll probably end up at Marten's."

She turned back to me and spoke to him over her shoulder without looking at him. "I said I'll give you a call."

"I'm just offering you a ride."

"If I'm going into town, I'll walk."

"Aw, come on. That's ridiculous," he said.

She spun around and raised her voice. "Why are you still here? I want to talk to Dr. Noonan. Get lost!"

Devon turned and marched to the door. As he stepped into the corridor, he said, "Bitch!" just loud enough for us to hear.

Kate turned back to me. "Sorry you had to hear that."

"Seems like it would be a long walk into town," I said.

"There's a shortcut through a field from College Avenue. It takes about forty-five minutes."

"At night? That doesn't seem very safe."

She smiled. "We do it all the time. It's no big deal. I wanted to ask you something. I noticed something kind of cool yesterday in the chapel. It might be a good idea for my paper. I don't know if I should bring it up in class or if I should talk to you about it."

"We can discuss it if you wish, but why not try writing down your thoughts about it first. You might be surprised by how far you can take it on your own. Then we'll talk about it."

Kate grinned. "Okay. I can do that. I know it will take some research. I might have to ask you for help on that part."

"That's okay. Scholars help each other all the time, just like Dr. Schumacher helped me yesterday."

Kate was nodding now. I could see that this was more than an assignment for her. It seemed she liked the idea that there were people who did this professionally. "I'm going to hit the library this afternoon and see what I can find. If I run into any snags, I'll shoot you an email."

"Sounds great," I said.

Saturday morning I woke up feeling I had a lot to celebrate. I had turned around my art history class and had gotten better acquainted with some of the students. The more I looked at the mural, the more it seemed worthy of scholarly attention. Jacob seemed willing to be a mentor to me when it came to the history of the institution. I had widened my social circle on campus, and that circle now included a man who was willing to spend most of the day with me hunting for good food and good art. I started to believe I could enjoy spending a year or two on this little campus.

Now, if only I could decide what to wear for our trip to Columbus. It couldn't be the business casual I wore to teach every day, but it couldn't be too dressy since it was an afternoon date. My options were limited since I had brought little with me from home, intending to buy clothes appropriate for the cold weather ahead, and I hadn't yet gotten around to shopping. My green flare dress would be fine. I could add a shawl to shift the color palette, and wear some dressy shoes, for a change.

Accessorizing was well underway when my phone rang. The call was from a local number not in my contacts list.

"Good morning," said a baritone voice. "This is Sheriff Mason Adams, Edwards County Sheriff's Department, calling to speak with Dr. Nicole Noonan."

A call from the sheriff? Was he finally going to investigate the vandalism of my car? "Yes, I'm Nicole Noonan."

"Doctor, it's important that I speak with you this morning. May I see you at your office or at your home on campus around eleven o'clock?"

"I have plans to go up to Columbus this morning. What's this about?"

He hesitated a few seconds before answering. "Have you read the email that the dean of students sent to everyone on campus?"

The dean of students was involved? Had someone discovered that a student targeted me because of my race? "No. I haven't checked my email this morning."

"Well, if you wouldn't mind reading the dean's email, it will explain everything. I am sorry to insist, but this urgent. I have your office as room 333 in the Arts and Humanities Building. Will you meet me there at eleven?"

I agreed, hung up, and opened my laptop.

Urgent? Why would the sheriff and the dean treat this matter as urgent after doing nothing for almost a week?

The dean's email was written with professional detachment, as such messages always are. It hit all the right notes, giving an objective view of the situation, but there was no getting away from the terrible news it brought. Kate Conrad was dead.

Chapter 5

Back in my bedroom my dress lay on the bed. The shawl . . . the purse . . . the shoes . . . Why had I worried about such trivial things?

I couldn't believe what I had just read in the dean's email, so I read it again. " . . . inform you of the death of Kate Conrad . . . investigation by the county sheriff . . ."

My gut felt all watery. I sat on the side of the bed, rubbed my face with both hands, and took deep breaths. That seemed to help the nausea.

Healthy young women don't just die. Sure, there are rare diseases, and exotic infections, and lightning can strike, but . . . Kate?

I read the dean's email again. It said nothing about how she died.

After class yesterday, when Devon tried to make a date with her, Kate said she might walk into town. Maybe she was hit by a car.

I had to know.

I called the sheriff. "The email says a student died but doesn't say how. What happened?"

"I'll explain that when I meet with you."

"Was there an accident on the highway?"

"Dr. Noonan, we like to have these conversations in person. I will see you at your office at eleven."

I felt a fury rise from inside me. "I'm sorry, Sheriff. That's not a good time for me."

"Doctor, I'm sure you understand that law enforcement

officers depend on cooperation from the citizens we're trying to protect."

"Why can't you just answer my question?"

"If eleven o'clock doesn't work for you, I could come by at ten."

He sounded bored. There was no way to make a dent in him. "All right. I'll be at my office at ten."

I hung up and called Lionel. "Would you mind if we left for Columbus at eleven instead of ten? We could still have a late lunch at the museum's cafe."

"That will be fine," he said. "Are you feeling alright? You sound a bit—I'm not sure—perplexed?"

"I just got a call from the county sheriff. He needs to speak with me. Have you seen the email from the dean of students?"

"Yes, about the death of that student. Did you know her?"

I had to clear my throat before I could say, "She was in my art history class."

"I'm so sorry, Nicole. Are you sure you feel up to our trip today?"

"I'm not sure about anything right now, but I think it would do me good to get off campus. I need to spend some time in a city."

"All right, then. I'll pick you up at eleven."

While doing my hair and makeup for the day, I remembered the cheerful way Kate called out, "Hey, Dr. Noonan!" She enjoyed learning and she enjoyed life. How could that have ended?

I needed answers. I needed something to make sense. I threw on a sweater, jeans, and running shoes and headed out to meet the sheriff.

My office on the third floor of Arts and Humanities had a window overlooking the downward slope of a wooded hillside. Sitting at my desk, I saw some pale-yellow spots among the wave of green treetops, my first glimpse of autumn color.

I had just fired up my laptop and was trying to keep myself busy when I heard a knock. I looked up to see a man the size of tree trunk standing in my doorway. Almost everyone looks tall to me, but even allowing for that this man was mighty impressive.

"Dr. . . . Noonan?" He got points for originality: putting the five-second stare between "Doctor" and "Noonan."

"Yes," I said. "Have a seat."

"Thank you, ma'am. Sheriff Mason Adams, Edwards County Sheriff's Department."

He took the chair next to my desk, looked for a place to put his hat, and ended up resting it on his lap. Even sitting down, he looked tall.

"How can I help you, sheriff?"

"We're investigating the death of Kate Conrad. The dean of students said you were one of her professors and gave me your name and phone number."

"Yes. Kate was in my art history class."

The sheriff wrote in his notebook before speaking again. "Now then, we would like to know anything you can tell us about her work as a student, her friends, activities on campus, and so forth."

"How did she die?"

"Until we've completed our investigation, I can't say. . . ."

"Where was she found?"

The sheriff raised his eyebrows, and I had a feeling he did not do that very often. His crew cut, clean shave, crisp uniform, erect posture, and rock-solid physique suggested he could have been on a Marine Corps recruiting poster twenty years ago. "All of that information will be made available through the department's public information officer. Now then, how many students are in this class of yours?"

Abbie had told me that in this rural county people at the college, especially professors, were treated with extra respect. I decided to test that theory. I cleared my face of expression and stared at the bridge of the sheriff's nose, certain I could wait as long as he could.

He glanced away and looked out at the hillside below my office window. "Dr. Noonan, I'm asking for your cooperation."

"Cooperation means we work together."

He kept his eyes on the woods outside as he considered his options. "The victim was found lying along Route 212 early this morning. A local farmer saw the body, stopped, and called 911."

Route 212 was the continuation of College Avenue after it left campus. "Was she close to a footpath that crosses a field?"

"Yes, ma'am. She was about thirty yards from there. Now, I think you'd better tell me why you would ask that."

"Some students use that as a shortcut to walk into Blanton."

"I'm aware of that. Do you have reason to believe the vic . . . uh, Ms. Conrad may have used that path last night?"

"Yesterday afternoon, I heard her tell another student she might walk into town in the evening."

"Who was this other student?"

I hesitated, unsure about whether to put Devon on the sheriff's radar, but sensed that refusing to name him would arouse greater suspicion. "His name is Devon Manus. He's also in my art history class."

"Did there appear to be any reason why she would have told him this?"

"He had offered her a ride into town along with some of their friends."

"So a male student, Devon Manus, offered her a ride into town last evening, and she said she would prefer to walk?"

"That was the gist of it."

The sheriff read over what he had just written before asking, "Were they arguing? Did they seem angry with one another?"

"I think that's fair to say."

"How well acquainted were they?"

"I only met them two weeks ago when classes started, but I had the impression there was a romantic relationship or maybe the beginnings of one."

The sheriff made notes. "Was Ms. Conrad enrolled in any of your other courses?"

"No."

"Did you ever hear her speak about any other students she may have been friends with?"

I'd had it with the guessing game. "Sheriff, I don't understand why you're asking about everyone she knew. How will that help you find out who was driving the car?"

"Which car is that, ma'am?"

"The car that hit her."

"Why do you believe she was struck by a car?"

"I . . . Isn't that what happened? You said she was lying along the road. If she was walking back to campus at night . . ."

The sheriff closed his notebook. "We haven't determined the cause of death. Until we do, it would be best not to start rumors. That can only make our job more difficult." He got up to leave.

I stood up too, and that's when it became clear I was about eye-level with the badge on his chest. "But you can tell from the condition of the body if she was hit by a car, can't you?" I stood as straight as I could and crossed my arms over my chest, doing my best to look imposing.

He looked down at me for a moment, and his official pose seemed to soften just a bit. "There was a massive head trauma. That appears to be the only injury, but that's for the medical examiner to decide. Until he does, there's no use guessing about what killed her. I would ask you, please, do not circulate that bit of information."

He thanked me and left.

If a person were hit by a car and knocked down, her head would hit the pavement, but how could she not be injured anywhere else? It sounded more like someone had deliberately struck Kate. The idea that someone had killed her—that she had been murdered—made this so much worse. I felt sick to my stomach.

Something else about this conversation with the sheriff bothered me. When I gave him Devon's name, he didn't ask me to spell it, and he didn't pause before writing it down. He must have already heard it from someone else.

Chapter 6

I was dressed and waiting when Lionel parked in front of my Rabbit Hutch and got out of his car, looking sharp in gray slacks, a lemon yellow knit shirt, and a blue blazer. If not for the catastrophe of Kate's death, a trip off campus with this man would have sent my spirits soaring.

His eyes scanned the small, wood-frame building, and he smiled as I walked out to meet him.

"This takes me back," he said.

"In a good way?"

He considered that for a moment. "I am not unhappy with what I was able to make of those years."

I'm sure there was great truth to what he was saying, but my brain wasn't up to it just then.

We left the campus on College Avenue. Where it became Route 212, I looked to the right so I could see where the path across the field joined the road. When I saw it coming, I looked to the left and caught a glimpse of crime-scene tape on the saplings that grew on the other side.

Lionel pulled over at a wide spot covered with gravel.

"Why did you stop?" I asked.

"Was there something you wanted to see back there?"

I turned and looked out the rear window of the car. "The sheriff said she was found back there, lying along the road."

Lionel turned the car around, drove back, and stopped near the path. We got out and walked to the spot marked by the tape.

There were lots of footprints in the dirt alongside the road but not much else. I wasn't sure what I had expected to see. Still I was glad I had come to this spot where she breathed her last. I took a quiet moment to remember her enthusiasm, her intelligence, and her innocence.

When I started back to the car with Lionel, an alarm went off somewhere in the back of my mind. "Something's wrong," I said.

Lionel turned to me. "What is it?"

"Why was she walking on this side of the road?"

Lionel looked back and forth, assessing the situation. "I don't know."

"It was after dark. She should have been walking on the other side of the road, so she faced the oncoming traffic."

He nodded. "She might still be alive if she had."

"No. What I mean is, she had no reason to cross to this side. If she came from the path over there, she would have turned left and started walking toward campus on that side of the road. It would have been simpler, and it would have felt safer. Why would she bother to cross to this side of the road?"

"Maybe someone in the woods on this side called out to her, and she came over to join them."

"That's possible, if it was someone she knew."

"Or maybe a car came along, headed toward the campus, and the driver offered her a ride."

"Also possible, and again it would have to be someone she recognized. That means she probably was killed by someone she knew."

"You think someone killed her?"

I remembered the sheriff's warning not to repeat the information he had given me. "I don't know. Let's get in the car."

Lionel found a driveway, turned the car around, and again drove away from campus, toward the highway. "What are you thinking?" he asked.

"I don't know what to think."

We were quiet during the rest of the drive into Blanton.

As we drove down Main Street and crossed Brook and Maple, I found myself scanning the sidewalks to see if Huey Littleton was around. If he stopped dead in his tracks at the sight of an Asian woman in "his" town, I hated to imagine how he might react to an Asian and an African-American in a car together.

"You've had a very hard week," said Lionel.

After a sigh I said, "Until this happened, it was a good week. I met my art history class in the chapel to study the mural, and the students responded to it really well."

"I'm glad to hear that. What I meant was this tragedy comes on top of having your car vandalized. Two traumatic experiences in a few days is a lot to absorb."

"Now that you mention it, I should have asked the sheriff about my car. But it doesn't seem so important now. I can't believe I was so upset about it earlier in the week."

"I can see why you were. You were the victim of a crime. Frankly I'm feeling a bit anxious about two violent incidents in our community in just a few days. In my three years at Fuchs, nothing like either of these has happened. I'm starting to ask 'Why now?' though I know there's no answer. These things occur randomly."

Lionel's question resonated deep inside me. "Now that you mention it, my car got vandalized, and my race insulted, and Kate was my student. I seem to be the common element."

"I didn't mean to suggest that," he said. "No, you shouldn't think this is about you. The tagging and the race-baiting perhaps, but not the death of this student. That was probably a hit-and-run, the kind of thing everyone has worried about for years with students walking into Blanton at night."

But if it wasn't an accident—if Kate was murdered—I faced the horrifying possibility that someone, who did their best to make my life miserable by spray-painting my car, also went so far as to take a student's life just to . . . To do what? To scare me off?

"You're right," I said to him. "I'm probably overreacting. Maybe we should talk about something else."

As we drove up to Columbus, we had the usual getting-acquainted conversation, academic edition. He told me he was from New York City, specifically Harlem. His family had lived there for four generations. He went to Howard University and did his graduate work at the Sorbonne in Paris.

I was equally forthcoming, describing myself as the daughter of a Chinese-American mother who worked as a librarian for the San Francisco Public Library, and an Irish-American father who worked in construction. After graduating from San Francisco State, I went on to the University of California, Santa Barbara, for grad school.

Lunch at the museum cafe overlooking the sculpture garden was like breathing pure oxygen. After lunch, we walked through the permanent collection, and I made mental notes to return. I liked the way they hung the work of local artists alongside that of recognized masters to invite comparison. The collection was especially rich in the works of George Bellows, who is both a native of Columbus and widely recognized.

After the museum, we drove to a neighborhood called the Short North, where our tour of Lionel's favorite gourmet food shops left me giggling with delight. At his suggestion, we stopped at a neighborhood Italian restaurant for an early dinner. I was surprised at how hungry I was.

I felt a deep satisfaction as we negotiated the freeway interchanges and got back on Route 23, headed south. We discussed paintings in the museum and scenes from favorite films, allowing comfortable silences in which our thoughts could ripen.

After we bypassed Chillicothe, the lights from towns became fewer and farther between, and it felt like we were driving into a dark tunnel. The isolation that came with living on a rural campus weighed more heavily on me than when we had set out that morning. The horror of Kate's death came back double.

When Lionel stopped the car in front of my Hutch, I said,

"Please come in for a glass of wine. It's the least I can do to thank you for a wonderful afternoon and evening."

Chapter 7

Lionel smiled before replying to my invitation. "That's a lovely thought, but . . ."

I saved him the trouble of thinking up an excuse that wouldn't hurt my feelings. "I'm talking about a glass of wine and a little conversation while you're not having to drive the car. Then I'll send you on your way."

He nodded. "All right then."

In the Rabbit Hutches, when you step through the front door you're in the living room, which is also the kitchen and dining room. One could call it a great room, but fifteen by fifteen is not all that great.

Lionel glanced around and smiled. "I love what you've done with the place."

What I had done was to furnish my Hutch on a budget with an eye to practicality. That meant a pair of canvas-sling beach chairs by the front window, a folding cafe table and two chairs by the back window, and two shelving units on the sidewall. Except for the floor lamp it was all outdoor furniture. With that in mind I had skipped getting a rug and instead had visited a large gardening store where I found artificial turf available in doormat-size pieces. I had stitched a few of them together and had a little green lawn in the middle of the room.

We hung our coats on hooks by the door, and I poured two glasses of wine while Lionel stepped into the other room to use the facilities.

When he returned and sat in the beach chair opposite me, I asked, "How do you do it?"

"Specifically?"

"Live here. You left New York, where you were a subway ride away from anything you could want. In San Francisco, I can take a bus or a streetcar to museums, festivals, theater, and baseball games, not to mention restaurants and every kind of store. Here, it's a long drive to Columbus, and when you get there it feels like you're just visiting. I thought going there today would help, but it only makes me feel more isolated."

Lionel tilted his head to one side and rested his eyes on my face. "I know what you mean. My first semester was like that. Think of it this way: When Thoreau moved to his one-room cabin at Walden Pond to live deliberately, he stayed two years; then he moved back to town."

I was going to have to get used to Lionel thinking on a plane I only glimpsed from time to time. When the further implication of what he said hit me, I asked, "So you're moving on?"

"I'm remaining aware of other opportunities. Meanwhile, my time of living deliberately has stretched to three years. I'm probably better for it, but I don't think of it as a permanent situation."

"I don't either, but the job market in art history is not encouraging."

"It's not encouraging in modern languages either." He sipped some wine. "Also, for what it's worth, you're doing a better job with your first semester than I did with mine."

"I can't imagine how."

"With your Rabbit Hutch, for one thing," he said, as his eyes swept the room. "It would seem you have a sense of humor about your situation."

"Well, yes, the artificial grass was a whim, but after losing Kate I'm not sure how many creative solutions I have left in me."

"I've never lost a student that way," said Lionel. "I can't imagine what it's like."

"She was extraordinary. When I was a teaching assistant, I saw hundreds of undergraduates during office hours and helped them write their papers and prepare for their exams. Most of them just wanted to know what they had to do to get a grade. Only a few of them showed curiosity about the subject and an eagerness to look further." As I spoke I felt my spirits sink. "I've already beat the odds by getting one like that in my first semester of full-time teaching. What are the odds of getting another one anytime soon?"

"Maybe better than you think. Good teachers attract good students, whatever the subject."

"Thank you. I hope you're right. I just noticed how selfish I sound. Kate lost her life. Her parents lost a daughter. Compared to that, losing my star pupil is a minor disappointment."

"Would you feel the same if you had just found out she was transferring to another school?"

Good question. "I'd still be disappointed, but I'd be happy for her if she had a better opportunity."

"So you're not being selfish. You're feeling both her loss and your own disappointment."

Everything about this conversation made me want to spend more time with Lionel.

He drank the last of his wine. "Please call on me if you need to. Will you be alright?"

"Thank you, I'll be fine. I'll probably call home tomorrow. Talking to Mom and Dad helps me see the big picture. And there's Abbie. Do you know her? Abbie Krauss?"

Lionel nodded. "Yes. I got to know her when I lived in the Rabbit Hutches. I like Abbie."

"She's been a real friend from day one. I don't know how I would have gotten started here without her."

"I'm glad to hear it," said Lionel as he stood up.

I stood up too and had to hold on for a second. The wine had gone to my head.

Lionel plucked his jacket from the hook by the door and

folded it over his arm. "This has been delightful. We'll have to do it again."

"Yes. Again, soon,"

He left.

As I got ready for bed, I was glad he let me know he was "remaining aware of other possibilities," job-wise. Obviously that meant we weren't starting a serious relationship. If he hadn't been clear about that, I might have found it easy to get attached to a guy who took good care of himself, appreciated the finer things in life, listened carefully to what I had to say, and looked upon his fellow human beings with kindness and generosity.

On Sunday morning I called Mom and Dad as I had every Sunday morning since moving to Ohio.

"Hi Nicole," said Mom. "Wait a minute. I'll get your father. Terry! Nicole's on the phone."

I waited, listening to footsteps and chairs being pulled out at the kitchen table.

"Okay, honey, I'm going to put you on speakerphone now."

All my phone calls with them started this way.

"How'd your classes go this week, darlin'?" asked Dad.

"Much better, Dad. The students really liked the mural. It got them thinking. And it got me thinking too. I might write an article on it."

"Now, you see, Linda?" I could tell Dad had turned away from the phone to speak to Mom. "I told you. The girl's a genius. By this time next year she'll be in charge of the art department."

Although I couldn't hear it, I knew that Mom was patting Dad's hand to make him settle down. "Nicole, Honey, how are you? You sound a little down."

"Well . . ." I choked up and cleared my throat. "I am pretty upset. Yesterday morning I found out one of my students was killed Friday night."

After a few seconds of silence, Mom asked, "Do they know how it happened?"

"Not yet. She was walking back to campus at night. Students go into town on the weekends. She might have been hit by a car. She was found lying by the road yesterday morning."

"Oh, honey, I'm so sorry."

Dad said, "I don't see how the college can allow students to be out walking along a road at night."

Mom replied for me. "Terry, they can't lock them up."

"That's not what I'm saying," he said, "but there has to be a way."

"Actually, Dad, sometimes the students drive into Blanton. In fact I heard another student offer her a ride, and she turned him down."

"Well, there you are. You make a rule: No walking into town. Go by car only."

Now I actually could hear Mom patting Dad's hand. "Honey," she said to me, "Don't try to handle this all by yourself. Have you talked to your friend about this? What's her name?"

"Abbie. She's in Pittsburgh this weekend, but I've already talked about it with Lionel."

The silence this time was longer than when I told them my student was killed.

"I'm sorry, honey, with whom?"

"Lionel Bell. We drove up to Columbus yesterday and visited the art museum and did a little shopping."

"Is this someone you met on campus?"

"Yes. He's a professor too. He teaches French."

"That's wonderful, darlin'," said Dad. "I'm glad you're dating again."

"It wasn't really a date." I decided not to mention we had dinner.

Mom said, "He sounds very nice."

"Mom, all I said was he's a French professor. You don't

41

know anything about him."

"I meant it was nice of him to go up to the museum with you. Are you seeing him again?"

"We haven't made plans yet. I'll let you know."

"How's your car running?" asked Dad.

When I got the job at Fuchs, Dad went online and bought me a used car from a dealer in Columbus so I could take a cab from the airport and pick it up. He insisted it was a present for finishing my PhD. I insisted I would pay them back once I was earning a regular salary, but, unless I learned to stretch my paycheck further, it was going to be a gift.

"It's running great, Dad, but I do have one problem. Monday morning, as I was leaving for class, I noticed somebody used black spray paint on the hood."

"That's terrible," said Mom.

"That's too bad," said Dad. "I wouldn't have thought there'd be much of that living way out in the country like you are."

"No," I said. "In fact, Lionel said he'd never heard of it happening on campus, and he's been here three years."

"Alright then, I'll tell you what to do." At moments like this, Dad sounded like a coach rallying the team. "Take your car to a place that does auto detailing and get it buffed out properly. You have to protect the finish. Get an estimate and I'll send you a check."

"That's not necessary, Dad."

"No arguments. In fact, I'll call a shop here in town and get an idea of what it costs. I'll send a check today. If it's not enough, you let me know."

"Okay. Thanks."

"Nicole, honey," said Mom, "I don't understand. Were other cars vandalized?"

"Not that I know of."

"So just yours? Why would someone pick your car?"

After hesitating, I decided it was best to get it over with. I held the phone away from my ear and said, "Well,

I'm the only Asian on campus, and whoever did it used the spray paint to write 'JAP OUT.'"

Chapter 8

Mom's voice shifted into operatic mode. Even through my phone's tiny speaker, it was deafening. "Oh, my god, Nicole! Have you called the police?"

"Campus security. Yes."

"They're not real police."

"Yes, they are mom, and they're right here on campus."

"What are they doing about it?"

"They're patrolling the area and checking for reports of other incidents."

"I mean, what are they doing to protect you?"

"That's all they can do, Mom."

"That's not good enough. You're not safe there, Nicole. If somebody wants you out of there, who knows how far they'll go?"

Dad's baritone voice came through the phone, sounding especially mellow. "What's the name of the head of security there, darlin'?"

"Why? What are you going to do?"

"I'm going to call your Uncle Pat."

"Dad! No!" Dad's brother, Pat, was a twenty-year veteran of the San Francisco Police Department.

"He can talk to your man there on campus. He'll know what to say."

I stifled my panic and did my best to sound reasonable. "No, Dad, I don't think that's appropriate."

"It's just a professional courtesy. They do it all the time."

"No, they don't, Dad. I'm pretty sure no cop in San

Francisco has ever called a campus security officer in Ohio to tell him how to do his job."

"That's not what I'm saying, darlin'."

Mom came back on the line. "Nicole, honey, you can't expect us to do nothing. We have to know your safe."

"I'm safe."

There was a pause, during which, I knew, Mom and Dad were looking at each other silently deciding who would make the next move. Mom won the toss.

"Nicole, you know your father and I have supported you in studying art history."

"We just want you to do whatever makes you happy, darlin'."

I leaned back in my chair, resigned to what was coming. "Yes, I know."

"We even supported you moving to Ohio for this job, even though it means we hardly ever see you."

"I know, Mom. You two have been really great about it."

"But now, I think, we need a different plan."

I knew exactly what the different plan was, but there was no point in saying so, because I was going to hear about it again no matter what I said.

"Honey, you could come back here and go to SF State. With all the education you already have you could probably get a degree in computer science or something in two years, and there are jobs all over the Bay Area begging for someone bright and creative like you."

"I know, Mom. We've had this conversation. I like art history. Since I'm just starting out, this was the only academic job I could get. I won't be here forever, but it's a start."

"But you could do your art history here. There are the museums and the galleries downtown. You could work part time while you're going to school."

"Mom, I like research. And that means an academic job. At least for now."

"Honey, just promise me you'll think about it. You could

have the in-law suite downstairs. That way you'd be independent. We wouldn't bother you."

Maybe there would come a day when Mom and I would compare notes on the meaning of the word "independent," but this was not that day. "I promise I'll think about it. I have to go now."

"Alright, but don't wait until next Sunday to call."

"I won't, Mom."

"Your mother's right, darlin'. We have to know you're safe."

"I'll call and let you know I'm safe."

After several more rounds of reassurance, we all got off the phone.

Although that blew up in my face, I was glad I'd told them. Deep down, I'd known they would overreact, but that was okay. It felt good to know they cared so much. And they weren't wrong. I couldn't let myself be a sitting duck.

To stop thinking about it, I gave myself something to do. I wrote a letter to Kate's parents, introducing myself, saying she was a brilliant student and a delightful young woman, and expressing gratitude for knowing her if only for such a short time. I told them that, though I couldn't imagine the depth of their grief, I was grieving her loss as well. Like all such notes, it seemed inadequate. I hoped it would bring them more comfort than pain.

Class on Monday morning was tough. With Kate gone, there were ten students left in my art history class, and only nine showed up. Devon wasn't there. I didn't recall anything from my graduate seminars about what to say when one of your students has died, especially when the class is small enough for everyone to notice.

I began by saying, "By now you have all heard of the death of Kate Conrad." I saw a range of reactions on their faces. Some looked sad and glanced toward the chair where Kate had sat. Others were curious about where I was going with this. When I said, "We will miss her contributions to our discussions," one of them gasped. Apparently, she had just figured out that the student named in the dean's email was one of the two absent from class. Ursula Wilmot sat ready as always to take notes, her eyes focused on something outside the window. She seemed to be waiting for me to get through this and get to work.

I fell back on the old chronological survey method. We talked about the Greeks and Romans, I showed some slides, and pointed out some important passages in the textbook (hint: this will be on the test). Ursula Wilmot was smiling by the end of class.

As I packed up after class, Byron Hawley approached, his t-shirt decorated with fresh evidence of his labors in the painting studio, and said, "I heard your car got spray-painted."

I wondered if gossip really did travel faster on a small campus than it did at a large university, or if it only seemed that way because it had less distance to travel. "Yes," I replied. "Do you know anything about that?"

"No. I just heard about it from some people in the department."

"I see. And why are you bringing this up?"

"I can help you with that," he said.

"Do you know of a place where I can have it removed?"

"I can remove it for you."

I stopped packing and took a fresh look at him. "Have you done this before?"

"Yeah, a couple of times. I've done some street art. Some guys accused me of painting over their mural, which wasn't true. Well, actually one time I did. Anyway, they tagged my car, and I got it off with acetone."

"Does that damage the car's finish?'

"No. It's basically nail polish remover. You have to be careful not to go too far, but it's really not a problem."

When he said, "really not a problem," I heard "might be a problem." "Thank you," I replied, "but I think I should have this done professionally."

He shook his head. "They're going to charge you an arm and a leg."

"I'd rather not risk it."

"Really, there's no risk. You can look at my car. It's in the student lot. The finish is fine."

If that was true, this was worth considering "How much would you charge?"

"I wouldn't charge you anything. I don't know how much spray paint you have on there, but I'm sure it would take less than an hour."

"Byron, it's very nice of you to offer, but I can't let you work for me for free."

He looked away for a moment as if deciding whether to go on. "I want to do it for free because I heard what they wrote on your car, and that's not right. You're new here, and I don't want you to think we're that kind of school."

This attitude was refreshing, but I didn't want to take advantage of him. "I'm not sure it was a student that did it. In fact, I doubt it."

"It doesn't matter who did it. We have to stand up to it as a community."

I certainly didn't want to discourage that kind of thinking, and I hated the thought of paying an arm and a leg. "Are you sure you can do this without damaging the car's finish?"

"Absolutely."

"Thank you, Byron, that would be great." I felt as if a weight was lifted from my shoulders.

I told him where my Rabbit Hutch was, and he said he would come by the next afternoon.

I dragged myself back to my office and called the shop in Chillicothe to cancel the appointment I had made to have them restore my car's finish.

I'd just hung up the phone when Devon appeared in the doorway. He was transformed. His face was slack and he looked off balance. "Can I talk to you, Dr. Noonan?"

Chapter 9

"Of course." I said to Devon and pointed to the chair by my desk.

He closed the door, sat, and rested his gaze on the treetops below the window of my office. For a minute or so he said nothing. "I . . . um . . . you know about Kate?"

I nodded. "I am sorry, Devon. I know you were close with her."

His face collapsed, and I thought he might cry, but he took a deep breath and steadied himself. "I'm sorry I wasn't in class this morning."

"That's all right. Take care of yourself first. You can get notes from someone, and we can talk later in the week."

He nodded and picked at the cuticle on his thumbnail. When he looked out the window again, there was a flash of anger in his eyes. The fire went out, and his look of sadness returned. "The sheriff talked to me on Saturday," he said.

I waited.

His eyes locked onto me like a cat stalking its prey. "Did you tell him I was Kate's boyfriend?"

"I did. It wasn't a secret."

He looked away and relaxed a bit. "He wanted to know how we were getting along, and what time I saw her Friday night."

I waited.

He continued. "So, it's okay for now, but I have a problem."

"Devon, before you go any further, think about whether

it's a problem I can help you with. You can speak to a counselor here on campus. Anything you say to her is confidential. You're not as protected when you talk to me."

"But you knew Kate."

"It might be better to talk to someone who can be objective."

"I can trust you."

That was true, but he had no way of knowing that. He just wanted it to be true.

He went on. "I had a problem when I was in high school."

I glanced at the clock. I would give him five minutes, then call a counselor for him.

"I had a girlfriend, senior year. We drove out to a park. We were in my car, in the back seat, making out, and she said she wanted to stop. So, I did. We did. I said I would take her home.

"She got out on the passenger side, and I got out on the driver's side. She tripped and fell and hit her head—the side of her face, really—on the side of the car. I ran right over and helped her up. She was crying, I think because when she fell she got her dress dirty. So, since she was crying, I went to put my arms around her, but she put her hand on my chest, so I stopped.

"Just then this guy comes jogging toward us and yells, 'Is there a problem?' He was an older guy, maybe in his thirties, and bigger than me. So, I held up my hands, and said, 'No, no problem.'

"Then the guy walked right up to us, real close. So, I stepped over, half in front of Teresa, because I didn't know what he was going to do. He said, 'Step aside, mister!' like we're in the army or something. I said, 'Hey, it's okay. She's my girlfriend. She's just upset. She tripped and fell. I'm going to drive her home now.'

"Then the guy saw the scratches on her face, and he shoved me aside, and yelled, 'Back off, mister! Back away!' So, I took a couple of steps back and held up my hands. I said,

'It's okay. I just need to take her home.' He asked Teresa, 'Are you okay? Did he hit you? Did he push you?' She was crying the whole time.

"Then the guy whipped out his cell phone and called the police. When they got there, one officer listened to him and me. The female officer took Teresa over to the police car and talked to her. They wouldn't let us talk to each other. I'm pretty sure Teresa told them the truth, because at one point I heard her say, 'No, nothing happened!'—loud, like she was sick of the whole business and just wanted to go home.

"Then the female officer drove away with her. I don't know if they took her to the police station or just took her home. Another police car followed me home, and they came in and talked to my parents. When they left, my dad yelled at me. He kept saying, 'So that's your story? You're sticking with that?' I don't think he believed me.

"After that, my parents, her parents—everybody—said I couldn't ever talk to her again. Her dad is Tom Zannetti. He's a big shot in Mansfield. Since then, we never have talked. She went to Ohio Northern and I came to school here."

He stared at the floor, but he seemed to be gazing into the depths of hell. There are certain sculptures by Rodin that capture the kind of despair I saw on his face.

"Devon, I am sorry this happened to you when you were in high school. It sounds like you were treated unfairly. How can I help you?"

There were tears in his eyes. "If they find out I was accused of hurting Teresa, they'll think I killed Kate. What should I do? No one would believe me last time, not even my own parents."

"Is there a police record of the incident?"

"I'm not sure."

"Were you arrested?"

"I don't think so."

"Were you handcuffed? Taken to a police station? Fingerprinted? Photographed? Put in a cell?"

"No. None of that."

"Well, then you probably don't have an arrest record. That's good. I don't know if police departments keep other kinds of records, but if they do there must be laws about sealing records of things that happened when you were a juvenile."

"That makes me feel better. Still, if they find out. . . ."

"I don't know what else to tell you, except you should have a lawyer with you if the police want to talk to you again. Talk to your parents so they can help you."

He reacted as if he felt an electric shock. "Are you kidding? If my dad hears this, he'll think I did it both times."

That was the saddest thing I had heard all morning. I decided to try another angle. "Were you with Kate on Friday night?"

"I drove some of our friends into Blanton and we went to Marten's. Kate showed up later, but she wasn't really with me. We were all just hanging out together. She took off while we were still there."

"Then what happened?"

"Nothing. We left around eleven or so. I drove the others back to campus, dropped them off, parked my car in the student lot, and walked back to my dorm."

"So you don't know where Kate went when she left Marten's?"

"No. She would hardly talk to me. She was just blowing me off. I don't know why."

"Well, since your friends came back to campus with you, they can tell the police you were with them and not with Kate."

He nodded and stared out the window for a moment. "I guess so. Thanks, Dr. Noonan. I just needed to talk to somebody—somebody who would believe me."

"I'm happy to talk with you, Devon, but you still need someone on your side who can help you in case the police want to question you again. Maybe one of your friends could help you find a lawyer."

"Yeah, maybe. Thanks. I'll see you in class."

He left, and I sat there wondering what to think and feeling alarmed. I hoped he wouldn't be overconfident about his situation.

My cell phone rang. It was Abbie. "Hi, Nicole. I'm just going through my campus email. I was in Pittsburgh over the weekend. Have you seen this message from the dean, about a student being killed?"

"Yes, I have."

"I guess it was bound to happen with students walking along the road to Blanton at night, but still it's a shock."

"Yes. I'm really going to miss her."

I thought I heard a gasp before Abbie asked, "You knew her?"

"She was in my art history class."

"Oh, my god! I'm so sorry. How are you holding up?"

"Honestly, it seems to get a little worse each day."

"Do you want to have lunch?"

"I've got a one o'clock, and I need some time to get my head together for it."

"After? Make a run into Blanton?"

"Maybe just meet back at the Hutches."

"My place, three o'clock," she said, and we rang off.

Chapter 10

Abbie's approach to furnishing her Rabbit Hutch was the opposite of mine. She had a pair of easy chairs upholstered in brocade and some oak tables. Perhaps they were from her family's home, or she may have picked up some refurbished antiques. She made tea and we sat on a couple of cane-seat chairs at a pedestal table by her back window. The afternoon light was lovely on the trees beyond the lawn.

"A student walking back to campus at night is an accident waiting to happen," said Abbie. "Maybe the college will do something now."

"I don't think the sheriff is treating it as an accident."

"What do you mean?"

"Right before you called, a student was in my office, a guy named Devon Manus. Last Saturday, I mentioned him to Sheriff Adams because he and Kate had a disagreement Friday morning. Now the sheriff has questioned him about where he was Friday night, and Devon's afraid he'll be accused of killing Kate."

"Do you mean killing her in an accident or deliberately, as in murdering her?"

"He's afraid he'll be accused of murder because he was falsely accused of assaulting his girlfriend in high school."

Abbie sat back and thought about that for a moment. "What does the sheriff say about that?"

"He hasn't told the sheriff."

"So why did he tell you about it?"

"He wanted advice."

"What did you tell him?"

"I told him to talk to a counselor, talk to his parents, and talk to a lawyer."

"Is he going to?"

"Probably not."

Abbie scowled. "So he just laid his guilty secret on you?"

"Who says he's guilty?"

Abbie looked at me as if trying to read every shade of expression on my face. "Was there ever an abuser who didn't say, 'It was all a misunderstanding.'"

"You think he was lying to me?"

"I have no idea, but, if he does have a record of abuse, it would be to his advantage to spread the idea that he was falsely accused. That way, when the sheriff comes around asking questions, he'll find lots of people like you saying, 'Oh, that was all a mistake.'"

As usual, Abbie had a surprising interpretation of the facts. That was one of the things I enjoyed about talking with her, but in this instance I thought she had gone too far. "What you're describing is very calculating," I said. "It didn't seem that way, talking with hm. When I was a teaching assistant in grad school, I dealt with abusive students a few times. Devon didn't strike me as one of them. He seemed more scared than anything."

She shrugged. "Trust your gut."

"I think I'd rather use my head, and find out whether he's telling the truth."

"Why would you want to do that?"

"Because I know how it feels when someone attacks you without knowing anything about you."

Abbie thought about that for a moment. "Like when your car got sprayed?"

I nodded.

Abbie thought about that for a moment. "The sheriff is investigating. Won't he find out if this story about the high-school girlfriend is true?"

"I don't know, but I'm tired of waiting around for other people to look into who's doing what around here."

"What are you going to do?" she asked.

"I guess the easiest thing would be to ask the girlfriend if he hurt her."

"Do you think she would tell you?"

"I don't know."

"Do you even know who she is?"

"Devon said her name is Teresa Zannetti, and her dad is a big shot in Mansfield. Is that near here?"

Abbie shook her head. "It's somewhere north of Columbus."

"Still it shouldn't be too hard to find her."

"I guess not, but I can't imagine her opening up to a stranger about this."

"That will be the tricky part," I said.

We talked about the pros and cons of approaching the girlfriend but without more information couldn't come to a conclusion. Abbie gave me a hug and I left.

When I got back to my Hutch, I fired up my browser and searched for "Teresa Zannetti" on a few social media sites. I found her on BudStem, "The Buddy System." There were three women with that name, and one was connected with Mansfield, Ohio. She was fairly generous with her personal information, allowing anyone to see her class schedule, photos, and list of buddies, but she did not give an email address or phone number. To communicate directly with her, I would have to become her buddy on BudStem. I thought about sending her a request but doubted she would accept a complete stranger with no interests in common.

Since I couldn't think of a way to get in touch with her and convince her to talk to me, I decided to sleep on it.

I was glad for the President's Convocation scheduled for mid-day on Tuesday. Anything to break the routine was welcome. Apparently, the college had one every year, early in the fall semester. It gave the president a chance to speak to the assembled faculty about the school's situation and his plans for the year. It was his version of a State of the Union speech.

My chairman, Frank Rossi, had told me the art faculty usually met at the department's office and walked together over to the auditorium in the Old Classroom Building. He thought this made the department more visible to our colleagues. There were only two other professors in the department: Irving Zorn, whose abstract expressionist canvases sold for obscene amounts of money and decorated many corporate lobbies; and Wilma Halberstadt, who taught art education, which is a fine and necessary thing, though she seemed to put more emphasis on the education than on the art.

The four of us were sitting together when our president, Roland Taylor, took the stage. I had met him when I interviewed last spring. He could easily be cast in a movie as a college president or a CEO, and in fact he had been both, having previously headed a small manufacturing company in Indiana.

He began by mentioning the death of Kate Conrad, assuring us that the chief of campus security was cooperating with the county sheriff, and promising a review of safety and security policies by the end of the semester. He said all this in a conversational way before opening the folder he had with him and beginning his prepared remarks.

Since this was my first convocation, I didn't know if he always took a historical perspective, but he did that day. First he paid tribute to the independence of Felix Fuchs and the original members of the Eden Commune. Next he praised the vision of Hilda Kiefaber, who became the first headmistress of the Eden Independent School, which was established by the shareholders of the commune after the residential community was dissolved in the 1880s. Then he told how the school's governing board raised funds for buildings so that the school could become Fuchs College in 1920.

I was familiar with most of this from reading Jacob's

book, but I enjoyed hearing it as part of the convocation; a community that recalls its past when assessing its present situation is a healthy community.

His voice rose as he said, "Today I have the privilege of announcing that this institution is on the threshold of a third major transformation." He went on to say the college had begun negotiations with a donor interested in establishing a school of business and would soon launch a major fundraising campaign. Along with paying for a new building, the funds would be used to upgrade the library, improve the campus' computer network, hire additional faculty and so on. At the same time, he said, the college would begin to orient itself toward preparing students for careers while not in any way diminishing its traditional strength in liberal arts and sciences.

I was stunned. I had barely begun to understand who was who and what was what at Fuchs College, and it was changing.

Chapter 11

More than a hundred professors sat in silence as the president took a sip of water and shuffled his papers. When he spoke again, he did so in an intimate tone, as if he were speaking privately to each of us. "With the addition of a second school—a school of business alongside the school of liberal arts and sciences—we become a university. Members of our Board of Trustees have already spoken with officials in state government to clear the way for legally changing our designation from college to university when the new school of business opens its doors.

"Here we face an additional challenge, one less demanding than building a new school, yet no less vital to the identity of this institution. When we become a university, and are called a university, we know that the word 'university' will often be shortened to a single letter, U, in conversation, on t-shirts, and on other memorabilia. When we consider the tendency of English speakers to favor the shortened vowel sound over the long vowel sound—with which 'Fuchs' is properly pronounced—the problem becomes apparent. The name of our revered founder will not pair well with the abbreviation for university."

I had to hand it to President Taylor. Without saying it, he had made clear that no one would take seriously a school whose name sounded like an insult.

He continued. "Therefore, I call upon this faculty, which is the heart and mind of this great institution, to begin deliberations on a new name, a worthy successor to 'The Eden

Independent School' and 'Fuchs College.' I ask you, what shall we call this new university?"

With that he thanked us for our attention and departed the stage. Applause was lackluster. As my colleagues stood and walked up the aisles of the auditorium in pairs and threes, conversation was muted.

I followed Frank and the members of my department out onto the pavement in front of the building. There we hesitated, glanced at one another, and turned to our chairman, hoping for an explanation. "News to me," said Frank with a shrug. "Good news though. More people on campus. Critical mass. Vitality. Department meeting next Tuesday. I'll email you."

The members of my department went their separate ways, and I looked around at the dispersing faculty to see if Abbie or Lionel was available to talk. Instead I saw Jacob standing with four colleagues, all men about his age. I was not close enough to hear everything they were saying, but, from what I heard, they were arguing about the president's call to change the name of the school. When Jacob started to walk away, one of the others put a hand on his shoulder, and Jacob pivoted and backhanded the man. I couldn't tell if Jacob struck him in the face or merely batted his arm away, but the man seemed stunned, as were the others. "Never," roared Jacob. He charged across the pavement, and everyone made way for him.

I had spent ten years on university campuses, more than a third of my life, and I had never seen a physical altercation involving professors or graduate students. I had seen undergraduates fight, but only after a lot of drinking, and even then it was mostly shouting. That's why Jacob's single, angry gesture left most of us frozen in place.

As the others began murmuring to those near them, I felt conspicuous standing by myself. I hurried off to the Student Center, where I grabbed a sandwich and sat looking over the campus green while I ate.

The convocation and its aftermath left me feeling nervous. If other faculty felt the way Jacob did, changing the school's name would be an explosive topic. Also, despite Taylor's assurances that liberal arts would remain strong, a new emphasis on preparing students for careers did not sound good for me. If the school became financially strapped, as schools always did, majors that did not lead to jobs would be in jeopardy. If they started cutting programs to save money, they wouldn't even have an art history department to shut down. They could just turn me down for tenure in four years. All the more reason to keep looking for that next job.

As I walked to my office, I had an idea for getting in touch with Teresa Zannetti. It was possible someone she knew from high school in Mansfield had come to Fuchs College and enrolled in one of my classes—someone other than Devon, that is.

When I got to my office, I looked at the rosters for my three courses. There were thirty-five students in one section of art appreciation, thirty-three in the other, and ten in art history, for a total of seventy-eight. It took me a while to type each of those names into the search box on BudStem. By the time I was done, I had found two students from Mansfield, both from my afternoon section of art appreciation. I remembered seeing them in class, but hadn't spoken to them individually.

I sent a request to each of them, hoping they might like to be buddies with one of their professors. If they did, I would send a request to Teresa, and, if she knew either or both of them, she might agree to be my buddy. That was a lot of ifs, but it was the best chance I had.

Professor Jacob Schumacher lived in one of the Victorians on College Avenue, across and down a ways from the chapel. These were not grand pieces of architecture, but rather homes for a professional class of people in a style typical of the early 1900s. His two-story house had a square tower on one corner. The wide front porch and generous proportions promised comfort well beyond basic shelter. In other words, this house had nothing in common with the

Rabbit Hutches.

He answered the door wearing a brown suede vest over a black shirt, black slacks, and black shoes with pointy toes.

"Good afternoon, Dr. Noonan," he said.

"Please, call me Nicole."

"And you must call me Jacob."

He gestured toward the living room. "Please have a seat."

This was not in the same universe with the Rabbit Hutches: built-in bookcases along one wall, a bay window at the far end of the room with two wing chairs, armchairs and a loveseat clustered in front of a hearth, all under a high ceiling, and lit by casement windows with leaded glass. Part of my brain understood that he had been on the faculty here for probably thirty years, while I had been here about thirty days, but another part of my brain said, "Kill this man and take his house."

I sat on the loveseat and admired a collection of porcelain in a tall display case by the fireplace. There were two dinner plates and a few smaller plates, all painted with decorative borders and pastoral scenes. There were also teacups and saucers and a few figurines.

He smiled as he sat back and clasped his hands over his belly. "Do you like my collection of Meissen?"

"It's lovely," I said, "although I can't say I know much about it."

"Meissen is significant," he said. "In the early eighteenth century, they were the first Europeans to discover how to make white porcelain. Up to then it had to be imported from China."

"Very nice," I said.

Changing his, tone he said, "I want to offer my condolences on the death of your student. It must have been a terrible shock for you."

At that moment, I felt the shock as much as I had Saturday morning. "Yes, it was. Thank you."

"I know only what the dean put in his email on Saturday, and I'm afraid I'm not very good about following news reports. Is anything further known about how she died?"

"I'm not aware of anything," I said.

I decided to change the subject, because any further talk of this would bring me to tears. "I appreciate your offer to help with my research."

"I hope I can help. As I recall, you want to look in the archives for references to the mural?"

"Yes. In my dreams, I would find the artist's sketchbook so I could see how he or she collected images and developed themes. But, really, any mention of the artist or the mural would help."

"Of course. Let me give you a quick tour."

He picked up a laptop computer from the coffee table, navigated to a page, and handed it to me. On the screen I saw a page from the library catalogue. "All the items in the archive relevant to the years of the Eden Commune, 1851 to 1883, are listed as collections named for the families who donated them to the library," he said. "As you can see, there are quite a few. A single collection might give you a large number of documents. There's one, for instance, at the top of that page, a collection of letters written by a member of the commune between 1863 and 1869."

I clicked on the title of the item and saw that the file contained 104 letters, most on sheets measuring four and a half inches by seven inches. "I suppose it would take a few days to read them all," I said.

Jacob nodded. "That's right, and reading them would be the only way to know if the letters mention the mural, because only a few of these collections have been indexed. I've already checked those that are, and I didn't find a reference to the mural or to painting or artwork."

"So I would have to read through more than a hundred collections, each one containing perhaps hundreds pages?"

"Some more, some less." He took the computer from me, clicked on another entry, and handed it back. "This one, for instance, contains only a diary from 1877. It's a pocket-sized book, two inches by three inches, with forty pages."

"Still, there must be thousands of pages," I said. "Why don't we have the National Endowment for the Humanities give us an enormous grant to hire an army of scholars to index all these pages. If we hire enough of them, they could be done by Christmas."

Jacob chuckled. "If we could predict that somewhere in these documents is a cure for cancer or a formula for renewable fuels, I'm sure we could get the funding. A lost sonnet by Shakespeare might even do it."

His laugh brought on a fit of coughing. He turned away from me and pulled a handkerchief from his pocket to cover his mouth.

When he turned back, I noticed a spot of blood on his lower lip. "You have something on your lip," I said, touching my own lip in the same place.

Startled, he turned away again and wiped his lip repeatedly, checking his handkerchief each time. Apparently he wanted to make sure no more blood showed.

I made a few notes about the items Jacob had shown me. "Thanks for the introduction. Perhaps I'll spend some time reading through the catalogue entries to see if anything stands out for me."

Jacob nodded. "That's a good idea. And let me know if you have any trouble with the German. Some of the vocabulary is peculiar."

My mouth was dry and my heart was speeding up. "The German?"

Chapter 12

"Yes," said Jacob. "Most of the documents from the commune are in German. For instance, that collection of letters was addressed to relatives back in Germany. In general, members of the commune had little need for English. When they did business with English-speaking farmers from the area, rough translations sufficed."

When I was twelve, my family went to Lake Tahoe to stay with another family at a cabin. I had taken swimming lessons at Rossi Pool for several years, so I didn't hesitate to jump off a pier. By doing so, I learned that the water of a deep, mountain lake is frigid compared to the water of a pool in a neighborhood recreation center. Learning that the documents I wanted to read were written in German was a similar experience.

"Well, Jacob, I must confess, I do not read German."

"If something looks promising, perhaps I can help."

"I couldn't ask you to do that."

"I could at least glance at it or I might have an advanced student who would like to translate it for an independent study credit."

"That's very generous."

He shrugged. "It would also contribute to making the documents more accessible to others. Oh, there's one other thing to look for. Some of the documents are written in Gabelsberger."

"Gabelsberger? What is that?"

"It's a system of shorthand writing that was invented in

Germany in 1834. Some of the more literate members of the commune learned it before they came here. Paper was relatively expensive back then, so shorthand was used to avoid filling pages with longhand writing. It was also useful for recording a lecture or sermon."

"So I would have to get someone to translate the shorthand into German before I could have the German translated into English?"

"Yes. Gabelsberger hasn't been used since the 1920s, but I know of two scholars in Germany who can read it, although one of them is fairly old now."

I did my best to smile. "Jacob, I can't thank you enough."

"I hope I haven't discouraged you."

"Well, I had hoped for better news, but thank you for filling me in."

"You're welcome, and let me know how it goes."

As I left the building and walked back to my Rabbit Hutch, my feet felt heavy. My imaginary road that lead from Fuchs College to academic stardom was now blocked by an avalanche of German written in shorthand.

Maybe I could find an alternate route. When we met in the chapel, Jacob had mentioned that a building from the Oneida Commune still existed. I could find out if there was a mural there. I might also look outside the world of communes and see how many buildings survived in Ohio from the mid-1800s. One of them might have a mural. If its style matched the mural in the chapel, they might have been done by the same artist, who might be identifiable. I was speculating wildly, but often that kind of thinking can show you where to look.

When I came to the intersection of College Avenue and Ohio Avenue, the chapel was only a short walk away. I thought a few minutes with the mural might rekindle my enthusiasm for studying it.

The afternoon light from the west-facing windows was

spotty, and it shone unevenly on the mural, but there was enough to see the panorama of community life. I saw again the long noses of the farmer, the preacher, and the man in the orchard, which lead Jacob to suspect the muralist had depicted Felix Fuchs. It was a pleasure to revisit these images and themes, and to let my eyes skip around the mural, taking in more details.

I found it odd that in the preaching scene the preacher and congregation were shown with the exterior of the church in the background. Why wouldn't the muralist have shown them inside the church? Also between the preaching scene and the choir-singing scene was one in which men were completing the skeletal framework of a building. Why would that have been placed alongside scenes of worship? I pulled a notebook out of my bag and made a quick schematic drawing of this part of the mural. I also made a note to remind me to ask Jacob if he could meet me in the chapel on Thursday afternoon to take a look at these vignettes.

As I sketched and wrote, I felt calm. My brain seemed to unlock, and my thoughts flowed freely once more. I promised myself I would drop in here for an hour at least every other day, and collect my impressions. I got excited about moving forward with an article on the mural. Routine chores like grading quizzes, preparing classes, buying groceries, and even doing laundry began to seem possible once more.

I learned to do this when I was a girl. When Mom took me to the de Young Museum, about ten blocks from our house, I didn't want to leave. I started crying when she said it was time to go home. When we got home I used my crayons to make copies from memory of paintings I had seen at the museum so I wouldn't forget them. When I was older, I took art lessons and started studying art, but the real lesson from my childhood was that copying and thinking about a picture could make me feel better.

I went back to my office, revised my to-do lists, and checked the email in my Fuchs.edu account, which I hadn't opened in a few days. As I worked my way through the long list of messages, my fingers froze on the keyboard and I held my breath when I saw "Kate Conrad" in the sender column. I'm not superstitious, but for a moment I hesitated to click on the subject line, "My Research on the Mural," as if opening the message might unleash her ghost. I shook off the feeling and clicked.

> Hi Dr. Noonan,
> Just wanted to let you know I have a pretty good idea what I want to write my paper on. I got some good notes and sketches in the chapel yesterday afternoon. In the library today, I found some art history books that gave me some good ideas about what one of the coffins in the mural might mean. The bibliography in the back of the textbook was a big help and I found things online. Have a good weekend. I'll see you in class on Monday.
> Kate

I cried. All the fun of teaching Kate about art history, all her quick insight, all the writing she might have done, and the career she might have had, now were like a great cargo ship disappearing over the horizon. I had lost family members—an uncle and a cousin—and not felt this bereaved.

When I dried my eyes, I re-read the email and stopped at the word "coffins." I hadn't noticed any coffins in the mural. I made a note to look for them Thursday afternoon, when I would again have time to spend in the chapel. If I could find out what she was researching, maybe I could mention her work in a footnote when eventually I published something.

I slogged back to my Rabbit Hutch, ready to heal up from the shocks the afternoon had delivered by listening to some music, doing some exercises, and preparing a meal. Twenty yards from my front door, I stopped and looked. Something was different. My car. The hood was clear. No spray paint!

I hurried over and took a close look at it. No black paint remained. Running my hand over the surface, I felt no uneven spots. Byron Hawley had made good on his offer.

I choked up and felt tears in my eyes. Maybe a good deed could make up for a bad deed. Maybe I hadn't been a fool to move far from home to take his job. Maybe I'd call home this evening and let Mom and Dad know how this one turned out.

Wednesday morning class was uninspired. I took the conventional route, covering the material. The students seemed satisfied with conventional. Ursula Wilmot was in seventh heaven.

Around lunchtime, Sheriff Adams called and asked to meet with me again. I told him I could see him after my afternoon class.

Chapter 13

Sheriff Mason Adams arrived at me office at three o'clock. He really was as tall as I remembered. cHe wasted no time coming to the point. "Were you aware that Devon Manus has a history of abusing women?"

I took a moment to think about my answer, which must have made me look guilty. "I was not aware of it when we spoke on Saturday."

Now it was his turn to pause and think. "But you have since become aware of it?"

"Devon came to see me on Monday. He was upset over Kate's death, so I referred him to the counseling services on campus. He blurted out this story about how he was accused of abusing his girlfriend in high school."

Adams leaned toward me as he asked, "Why didn't you call me and tell me about this?"

I remained sitting straight up in my chair. "I didn't know whether he was telling the truth about it."

Adams kept the pressure on. "You do understand, Doctor, it is my job to determine whether people involved in a criminal case are telling the truth."

"I didn't know Devon was involved in a criminal case."

"I had just asked you about him on Saturday."

"When I spoke to you on Saturday, you wouldn't say whether she died accidentally or was killed deliberately. So I had no reason to think this was a criminal case."

He paused and leaned back. I could see his jaw muscles clench. "We now know her injuries are not consistent with being struck by a vehicle. We believe she was killed by a blow to the head."

Though it was not a total surprise, the sheriff's statement shocked me. "Well then," I said, "You seem to have found out about Devon's past without my help."

"The Mansfield police have been helpful."

"And what is their version of the story?"

"Instead, why don't you tell me Devon's version of the story?" he asked.

"Why don't you ask Devon?"

"I will. This is your chance to tell me your side of the story."

"I don't have a side," and paused when I noticed I had raised my voice. "I just want him treated fairly. He's my student. "

"I will treat him fairly. Right now all I have to go on is what the local police told me. Is there anything else I should know before I talk to him?"

Since he put it that way, I felt okay about sharing what I knew. "Devon told me he was out one evening with his high school girlfriend, and she slipped and fell. She got mud on her dress and scratched her face, and she was crying. A man came along and thought it looked like Devon had abused her, so he called the police."

Adams jotted a few notes as I spoke, and paused to look them over. "So Devon says he did not abuse his girlfriend, but this man assumed he did."

"Yes."

Adams rested his eyes on the woods outside my window. "That's possible. People are sometimes overzealous about calling the police, especially when it involves women or children." He closed his notebook and tucked it in his pocket along with his pen. "Thank you, Doctor. As I said, I'll talk to Devon. I'll approach the interview with an open mind."

71

"Sheriff, before you go, there's something else you might like to know. As I was leaving campus Saturday morning, I saw the crime-scene tape and I noticed it's across the road from the field where there's a footpath that goes into Blanton."

"That's correct."

"If Kate Conrad was walking back to campus on Friday night, it seems more natural that she would have turned left at the end of the path, and walked along the road facing traffic. She would have had no reason to cross the road and walk on the side where she was found unless it was to speak to someone she knew or accept a ride from someone."

Adams stared at the wall behind me as if visualizing the place where Kate died. "I see what you mean. Of course, in a murder investigation, we always start with the assumption that the victim knew her attacker because statistically that's most likely." When he looked at me again, his expression was softer. "But thanks for mentioning this. I hadn't thought of it."

"Also, Sheriff, Devon told me he drove a group of friends into Blanton on Friday night, and they spent some time at Marten's Tavern. He said Kate arrived after them, and left around ten. He and his friends left at eleven and he drove them back to campus."

The notebook and pen were out again before I finished speaking. When he finished jotting, he flipped back to an early page and compared it with what he had just written. "Thank you for mentioning that. I'll be sure to ask him about it."

"Sheriff, my point is, if Kate left Marten's around ten and started walking back to campus, she would have been on that road where she was killed while Devon was still at the bar."

When I finished speaking, he put away his notebook and pen. "I understand what you're saying. I'll be in touch." He stood up and held his hat in his hand.

"Excuse me," I said, "but do you know what time she died? Do you have the report from the medical examiner? Was she killed before eleven o'clock?"

Adams drew himself up to his full height. "Let me make

one thing clear, Doctor. You are cooperating with my investigation, not the other way around. Good afternoon." He left.

I shut my office door and walked to the window. There was more yellow in the treetops this week and a few hints of gold.

The sheriff seemed awfully defensive. I hoped he would take seriously the possibility that Devon had an alibi for the time of Kate's death. He could easily check by talking to the friends who were at the tavern with him.

Prompted by the sheriff's investigation of Devon's supposed history of abuse, I checked my Budstem account and found that one of my students had accepted my request to be buddies, but the other had not responded. I decided to wait and see if the other one would agree before sending a request to Teresa. If I couldn't reach her through BudStem by the end of the week, perhaps I could get in touch through her college.

Since Jacob agreed to meet me in the chapel at two thirty, I got there at two on that Thursday to see if I could find the coffins Kate mentioned in her email. As usual, the afternoon light from the east-facing windows was not the best, but I hated the thought of getting up hours before my morning classes to take advantage of morning light.

I looked over the parts of the mural I was familiar with but could find no coffins, which was not surprising in scenes about working in fields and orchards, preparing food, preaching, building, and singing. I used my binoculars to go over all these scenes in detail, knowing that muralists sometimes hide miniature objects among architectural details, decorative motifs, and so on. In particular, I looked at the spine of each hymnal held by a member of the choir in the singing scene, because each was marked to suggest a title printed there, but I found only lines and scribbles.

When I was satisfied there were no coffins hidden in the various scenes, I scanned the single, large tree whose trunk formed a symbolic background for the mural. Its leafy crown filled the triangular space where the wall extended to the roofline, and that was where I found the coffins. Five of them were clustered in a dark spot among the leaves.

To the naked eye they looked like shadows adding texture to the greenery, but when viewed through binoculars their six-sided shape became clear. They appeared open, as if the lids had been left off, and a human figure was visible inside each. Why would the muralist make the coffins so small and put them so far from the floor as to be practically invisible?

Jacob arrived, and I pulled a couple of chairs into the middle of the room so we could sit.

"Thanks for dropping by," I said.

Jacob smiled and nodded. "It's a pleasure. I am honored to be asked to assist with your scholarship."

"You gave me an important insight last week when you identified the preacher and the farmer as likely portraits of Felix Fuchs."

"I would never have thought about it—wouldn't even have bothered to look—if you hadn't asked the question."

At that point, I figured we had spent enough time patting each other on the back, so I moved on. "I wanted to ask you about the scene with the preacher. Why would the artist have shown Fuchs and his congregation outside the church? In that upper, left vignette, do you see how the exterior of the church appears to be in the background? Why wouldn't he show them inside the church?"

Jacob studied the scene before saying, "It might represent Fuchs preaching to his followers in Fellbach, their home in Germany. He would have preached outdoors there, because he was protesting the practices of the Lutheran church and wouldn't have been allowed in the pulpit."

Knowing that, the scene made sense. "I love the idea that the muralist put them outside the church physically to show they were outside the church theologically," I said.

"Of course, that's just a guess."

I took in the details of the church shown in the background. "What about that steeple? I don't remember seeing one like that anywhere around here."

Jacob nodded. "I don't know of one either. It certainly looks like the kind of steeple that is common on parish churches in Germany. I don't recall what the one in Fellbach looks like, but it would be easy to check."

I made a note to search images online for the parish church in Fellbach and its steeple. "If it's a match, that would support your idea that the artist was representing the commune's origin in Germany. And, if the preaching is taking place in Germany, I suppose the next scene, where they're raising a building, must represent the followers building their own church here."

Jacob considered for a moment, and said, "Yes, we could read this row from left to right: Fuchs preaches to his followers in Germany, they build themselves a new home, here presumably, and celebrate by singing as a choir."

"If we keep this up, I'll have to add your name as co-author of my paper on this mural."

"That's really not necessary. You deserve credit for asking all the right questions."

I jotted a few more notes. "Jacob, I want to ask you about something else. Kate Conrad sent me an email on Friday afternoon, the day she died. Her message said she had an idea for writing a paper on the mural because she thought she knew what one of the coffins might mean."

"Coffins?" Jacob turned to the mural and scanned it. "I don't see any coffins."

Chapter 14

The afternoon had turned cloudy. "It took me a while to find them," I said as I handed Jacob my binoculars. "Look in the crown of the tree, left of center, about halfway down from the ceiling. There is a cluster of five coffins hidden among the leaves."

After several seconds, he said, "Ah, there they are." He lowered the binoculars and turned to me. "That's very strange."

"It's actually not all that unusual. For instance, the stained-glass windows in the gothic cathedrals of Europe have many details not visible to the naked eye. Also, muralists and painters often camouflage objects among the details of their pictures either as puzzles or as secret messages."

Jacob lifted the binoculars once more and looked at the coffins. "This would seem to be a symbolic suggestion that those who have died and been buried are on their way to heaven."

"That's a possible interpretation," I said though I didn't really think so. "I'll have to spend some time looking at them to understand what Kate meant when she wrote, 'one of the coffins.'"

Jacob's thoughts were far away for a moment. "I'm sorry I can't help you on this point."

"That's all right. You've given me plenty of help. If you think of anything, let me know."

"Thank you again, for sharing your work. I must be going."

"Thanks for dropping by."

Grateful though I was for Jacob's help with interpreting the upper row of vignettes in the mural—preaching, building, and singing—I couldn't help being disappointed that he had no useful insight regarding the coffins.

I looked again at the cluster of five coffins with a human figure visible in each. Clothing identified two of the figures as women and three as men. Other than the clothes, there wasn't much to distinguish one figure from another. I couldn't imagine which one Kate had in mind.

Maybe there were other clusters hidden in the crown of the tree, but my eyes were tired from looking through binoculars in dim light. I would have to come back and discover them another day.

On Thursday evening Lionel called and asked if I was free for another road trip on Saturday. I didn't even pretend I had to check my calendar. "What do you have in mind? Another trip to Columbus?"

"No. This is a bit more out of the way. Let's get an early start. We can be there for lunch and get back before dark. We'll see some fall color along the way."

"Sounds delightful. Does this place have a name?"

"Yellow Springs."

We agreed to leave campus at eight o'clock, pick up muffins and coffee at Emma's Deli in Blanton, and hit the road.

First I had to get through Friday with its morning and afternoon classes. To all appearances things were going fine—I lectured, provoked a little discussion, and reminded them about quizzes, tests and assignments—but I had a moment of panic in art history when one of the students asked about the assignment to write a paper on the mural. She said she had been over her notes, and had tried writing about it, but wasn't sure what she was supposed to say.

There was a perfectly good reason for this. After telling

them they would be writing a paper I had forgotten about the assignment and given them no further instructions.

I finessed my moment of panic by telling them I would have a hand-out for them on Monday, which would give them a method for developing their papers. I smiled as I said it, even though at that moment I had no idea what the handout would say. I had the weekend to come up with something.

I left my office around two thirty and headed for my Rabbit Hutch, feeling worn out. It had been a busy week. In addition to keeping up with my classes, I had counseled Devon, but I didn't know if I had done him any good. I had twice met with Sheriff Adams and shared some information, but I didn't know if any of it meant anything. I had attended my first convocation and learned that the college that hired me was in the process of becoming a different kind of place. I wasn't sure what that might mean for my career or me. The only bright spots seemed to be my two visits to the chapel and continued study of the mural. Kate's email had prompted that. Even now, the good student was inspiring her professor. Somehow I would find out what she had discovered.

Friday evening, I checked my messages on BudStem and was delighted to see that both of my students from Mansfield had agreed to be buddies with me. I sent a request to Teresa Zannetti, hoping she would see we had mutual buddies and agree to be my buddy. If so, I could write to her directly, but first I would have to think of a way to convince her to talk to me about the incident with Devon when they were in high school.

On Saturday morning Lionel picked me up and we stopped at Emma's Deli in Blanton to pick up breakfast to eat in the car as we drove to Yellow Springs. Emma was cheerful as ever. She didn't mind having people from the college visit her place, even ones who look a little different.

We drove north, and, when we came to Chillicothe, instead of turning up Route 23 toward Columbus as we had last weekend, we stayed on Route 35 heading west. The rolling hills bordered by woods and creeks gave way to flat lands cut into rectangular fields by lines of trees left as windbreaks. It wasn't as pretty as the area east of Chillicothe, but as we drove through it freedom from the week's routine lifted my spirits.

After finishing our coffee and muffins, I asked Lionel if he had any ideas for changing the name of Fuchs College. He smiled and shook his head. "I suppose they could choose something that reflects the school's location, although naming it after Edwards County wouldn't mean much. Edwards University?"

"Couldn't they choose someone else from the history of the place, so the school doesn't entirely break from its past?"

"I suppose so," he said. "Hilda Kiefaber, the first headmistress of the Eden Independent School, would be a good choice. But no matter what they call it, focusing on education as career preparation will be a serious break from the past."

"Do you think that's a mistake?" I asked.

"I suppose it's a necessity. You can't expect people to go into debt paying for a college education unless it's going to help them earn more money. I just hope we don't completely lose sight of the idea that without the liberal arts—history, literature, art, science, philosophy—we don't have educated citizens, and without them we don't have a democracy."

I was ready to elect him to whatever he wanted to run for.

The rest of the way we compared notes on students, colleagues, and earthshaking issues such as new offerings at the snack bar in the student center.

I was surprised when our two-lane country road turned into Xenia Avenue, lined on both sides with shops, cafes, galleries, and restaurants. It reminded me of small towns like Healdsburg and Sebastopol in the wine country of Northern California. I hadn't seen anything like it in Ohio.

"Where are we?" I asked.

"Yellow Springs, home of Antioch College."

Chapter 15

It was like a corny joke. What do college professors do on their day off? Visit a different college. I had to admit though, this place was a revelation. The grand old building at the center of campus, a redbrick masterpiece with twin towers, put to shame anything at Fuchs. The newer buildings kept a low profile, as if content to allow the original building to set the tone. Like everything else in this part of the country, the buildings were dwarfed by lush green lawns and trees showing fall color.

After we toured the campus, Lionel drove us through a neighborhood of detached homes and back to Xenia Avenue. Along the way it was nice to see the Little Art Theater offering classics and foreign films, and a mix of stores for books, clothing, and local art.

He parked near the shops, and after a stroll we opted for lunch at a tavern that looked like it had been there a while. I ordered their seasonal special, squash soup and a salad. Lionel went for the chili burger.

"Cute place," I said. "Thanks for suggesting it."

"I couldn't have you thinking every small town in southern Ohio was like Blanton."

"Antioch College looks like it's doing well. Do they have a business school?"

"No, they're doubling down on liberal arts," he said.

"Really? How can they do that when we can't?"

"Probably because of their first president, Horace Mann. He believed education should be universal, free, and devoted to preparing people for citizenship. He was also an abolitionist. Yellow Springs became an important destination for the Underground Railroad."

"That's a wonderful history, but how does it help them keep their doors open?"

"Actually they have struggled in recent years, but for a century and a half they have been a magnet for people whose values are like Mann's. Therefore, they can draw on alumni to support the school in upholding those values."

"I see. Maybe Fuchs College should be calling on its alumni to uphold the values of its founder instead of adding a school of business," I said.

Lionel tilted his head to one side as he thought about that. "Maybe. There are people alive today who grew up hearing their grandparents talk about what life was like in the commune."

I thought of Jacob's history of the Eden commune, *Tree of Lif,e* which I had borrowed from the college library. "So what values would those be? I know Fuchs thought the clergy in Germany were acting like aristocrats, but that doesn't seem to have been an issue once he and his followers were settled here."

Lionel nodded. "Fuchs is a little hard to pin down. He wasn't a prophet like George Rapp, who also brought people from Germany to settle here, and he wasn't an intellectual like John Noyes who founded several communes before starting Oneida."

"According to Jacob's book, *Tree of Life*, Fuchs borrowed ideas from Noyes."

Lionel smiled. "I enjoyed *Tree of Life*. Jacob has a great feel for the material. Yes, Fuchs was influenced by Noyes. Also by the Shakers. They were more successful than anyone at creating communes. And then there were the phalanxes."

"The what?"

"Some communes were driven by religious reform, others by social and economic reform. The phalanxes were based on the philosophical writings of Charles Fourier." The name was French, so he said it with a French accent.

"Have you done research on him?" I asked.

"No, I'm just aware of his place in French letters. After the French Revolution overthrew the idea of a society based on aristocratic landowners and peasant workers, Fourier proposed replacing it with a society organized in phalanxes, which were four-story apartment complexes large enough to house a self-sustaining community."

"And Felix Fuchs knew about this?"

"Everybody did back then. In the mid-1800s, phalanxes were established from New Jersey all the way to Indiana. There were several across southern Ohio. Fuchs visited them and learned from them."

"I see why you say he's hard to pin down."

"I hear Jacob is at work on a biography of Fuchs. Who knows? Maybe he can convince us that Fuchs was a visionary like Horace Mann. Maybe that could help us keep some emphasis on the liberal arts in our new university."

"I'm so glad to hear you say that."

When we finished our lunches, we took a walk and visited at an espresso bar before hitting the road. On the way back, we stopped at a roadside stand to buy squash and a jug of cider.

Somewhere after that, I must have dozed off because the sound of the tires on the truss bridge across the river into Blanton woke me. "Oh, my goodness! I am so sorry. I'm usually better company than this."

"No need to apologize," said Lionel. I could hear the smile in his voice. "It's been a stressful week. It's good to see you relax."

We came off the bridge and drove a few blocks over to Main Street. "Lionel, do you feel comfortable in Blanton?"

"I'm not sure what you mean."

"When I come here to pick up groceries at Steadman's, or get something to eat at Emma's like we did this morning, I don't see any Asians other than the family that runs the restaurant. I also haven't seen many black people."

"There's a church across the river, and a few families live there, but you're right, not many."

"So, I wonder sometimes if minorities are welcome around here."

"We're with the college and the college is welcome here. They're happy to have us spend our money in their stores. So long as we keep to ourselves on campus and don't try to take over their town, they don't mind us."

"Abbie said there are unwritten rules like the one about who goes into which bar."

"That's true. There are lines you don't cross. I'm not planning to make Blanton my home, so I don't worry about it."

We fell silent as we turned up Route 212 and passed the spot where Kate had died. The crime-scene tape was gone from the side of the road. I felt a weight on my chest.

Lionel parked by the duplex where he lived on Ohio Avenue and we got out of the car. "Thanks for showing me Yellow Springs," I said. "This was a lovely day. I needed this."

"You're welcome," said Lionel. "Would you like to come in? I have some of that Roquefort left and a bottle of Medoc."

"You've already spent your whole day entertaining me. I don't want to take up your evening too."

"All right. I'll walk you back to your place."

"No need," I said. "It's just around the corner. I can practically see it from here. Thanks again. I'll be in touch." With that I was off down the road with a half-gallon of cider in one hand and a squash in the other. Though I wouldn't have minded a bite of Roquefort and a sip of Medoc, I was eager to get back to my place and check my Budstem account.

When I did, I found that Teresa Zannetti had agreed to be buddies with me. I went to her root page and found more information about her interests and activities on campus, plus an email address and a phone number. As a result, I knew a bit more about her, but I didn't see anything to suggest why the sheriff was reluctant to question her about the incident with Devon when they were in high school. I hated the idea that the sheriff would simply accept that Devon "had a history" without verifying it with the only person in a position to know.

I thought about calling her, introducing myself, and asking about that night when she was in high school and a man showed up to protect her from Devon, but that seemed like a bad idea. She would probably hang up. I know I would if I got a call like that. I thought about sending her an email, but decided that would be too easy for her to ignore.

I had a hunch that the best way to handle a sensitive matter like this was face to face, but off-hand I couldn't think of a way to persuade her to meet with me. I put the problem on the back burner of my subconscious, and looked up a recipe for making something with that squash.

For my Sunday-morning run, I tried something new. Instead of following Montgomery Avenue to Ohio Avenue, and Ohio to College Avenue, I went the other way on Montgomery and found it continued past the Rabbit Hutches, curved, and stopped at a grove of birches. There was a well-worn footpath through the trees, so I followed it. Before long I came out onto a gravel drive and saw the playing fields and gymnasium ahead. I continued running on this drive, knowing it would connect to the far end of College Avenue.

I was past the athletic fields when I saw a man walking toward me, about a quarter mile away. He wasn't jogging or carrying a duffel bag, so apparently he wasn't on his way to the gym. He was just strolling along in street clothes with his hands in his pockets and his head down.

When I had cut the distance between us in half, he must have heard my footsteps on the gravel, because he looked up at me and stopped. In the morning light, I saw only a silhouette. I got concerned when he took his hands out of his pockets, picked up his pace as he crossed to the middle of the road, and headed straight for me.

I had gotten out of the habit of wearing my rape whistle on a lanyard when I ran, having been lulled into a sense of security by the rural setting and the seeming safety of being on a campus. Now I didn't feel so safe, and I didn't see any place to get help if I needed it. I was on a half mile of road with the gym behind me and nothing ahead until I got to the far end of College Avenue.

I kept up my pace, and in less than a minute I could see this man more clearly. It was Devon, and he did not look happy.

Chapter 16

As I got to within several strides, I called out, "Hi Devon," looked straight ahead, and focused all my attention on running. I hoped this would make it clear I didn't intend to stop and talk.

He walked right into my path and yelled, "You told him."

If I ran around him he might chase me. Since I'd already been running for a while, I wasn't sure I could stay ahead of him. Instead I broke my stride and settled into a jog-in-place, still hoping to make clear that I wouldn't stop to talk. "Not a good time," I said between breaths. "Give me a call."

He acted like he didn't hear me. "Men from the sheriff's department came here and questioned me. You told them what I told you about my girlfriend in high school. I can't believe you would do that."

"No," I broke my rhythm and walked backward a few steps, resting my hands on my hips so I could breathe as deeply as possible. "The sheriff asked me about it. He already knew."

"How else could he find out if you didn't tell him?"

"From the police in your hometown."

Devon looked away for a moment. "I didn't think I had a police record."

"I imagine he called them and asked if you'd ever been in any trouble."

"Did you tell him what I told you?"

I didn't like the way Devon kept walking to within arm's

length of me. I did my best to speak calmly. "He said he wanted to know what you told me to balance what he heard from the police. He said he would keep an open mind. I think he's trying to be fair to you."

He shifted his weight from foot to foot and darted his eyes around as if he didn't know what to believe.

"Devon, you should be thanking me," I said, still catching my breath. "I told the sheriff you probably have an alibi. If Kate started walking back to campus at ten, she would have gotten to the road where she died before you and your friends left Marten's at eleven."

He looked hard at me, not grasping the implications of what I said.

I explained, "Your friends can tell the sheriff they were with you at the bar."

"Then why didn't he believe you?" Devon yelled. "He called my parents. I caught hell from my dad." Devon chopped at the air with his hands as he spoke, still unable to contain his frustration. "I had to talk him into letting me stay on campus."

I heard a crunching sound behind me. Devon glanced past me and looked scared. I risked a look over my shoulder and saw the campus security patrol car rolling slowly toward us on the gravel drive. We both moved to the side of the road. The officer drove alongside us and lowered the passenger window. He was a heavy-set man with black hair. "Everything all right here?"

After staring at me for a moment, Devon hurried toward College Avenue, taking long strides.

"Are you alright, Dr. Noonan?" asked the officer.

I had never even seen this officer, yet he knew my name. Of course he did. I was the only Asian woman on campus. Of the several new faculty, I was probably the one everybody knew by name.

I was hugging myself, and starting to shiver. "Actually, I'm a little chilly. Any chance of a ride over to Montgomery Avenue?"

He nodded and unlocked the passenger-side door.

As I stood in a steaming shower, I felt sorry for Devon despite our argument. Without support from his family, his father in particular, I couldn't imagine how he would get through this ordeal. At the same time, I had to resist trying to be a parent to him. He needed a counselor and a lawyer. Maybe I could make some phone calls tomorrow.

Having thought it over since last evening, I sat down with my laptop and took another look at Teresa Zannetti's pages on Budstem. A leaf attached to her current stem told me she was "super-excited" to watch the Bears beat Heidelberg on the coming Saturday. Ohio Northern University's website listed Heidelberg as a home game, so apparently she was staying on campus. That was good news, but, if I went there to meet her, I couldn't just show up with her picture on my phone and walk around campus looking for her. I would need some way to make her agree to meet with me.

Reading further down her stem, I saw a number of leaves about the show she hosted on the campus radio station. She had recently featured three students who wrote songs and performed on campus, and she had reported on regional festivals for new music.

I switched over to my personal email account and drafted a message, making up my story as I went along. I said I was a producer for NPR and that my team was putting together a feature on singer-songwriters who were breaking out with new recordings and appearances at larger festivals. I went on to say that one of these performers had mentioned how important college radio stations are for building an audience, and that I wanted one or two hosts of college programs to appear in the story. I asked if she would be available for a preliminary interview on Saturday morning since I would be near her campus on my way to some schools in Indiana.

I knew lying about this would be a semi-ethical thing to do and had to stop and ask myself if I really wanted to do it.

After all, it wasn't my job to investigate Devon's background. On the other hand, I knew how Devon must have felt when someone who knew nothing about him labeled him as evil. Seeing "JAP OUT" on the hood of my car had taught me that. I wasn't going to let Adams or anyone else label Devon an abuser unless they could prove it. So far as I could see, the only way to find out the facts involved approaching Teresa Zannetti under false pretenses.

I soothed my conscience by remembering I would be deceiving her for only about thirty-six hours, that the disappointment would not be huge in the great scheme of things, and that I was teaching her to be more careful about putting personal information online. With all that in mind, I clicked send.

My phone rang. It was Abbie. I saw she had left a voicemail a few minutes ago, when I was in the shower.

"You got picked up by the cops, eh?"

I laughed out loud.

She did not share my amusement. "Seriously, are you okay?"

"Sure. Why?"

"When someone is driven home by the campus police, I assume it's because they needed assistance."

"Oh, right. Yeah, I'm good. I was out running, and I ran into a student. Actually, that part was a little scary. Wait a minute, how did you know the campus police brought me back? I thought you were in Pittsburgh."

"I was. I came back early. I was looking out my front window when the cop car dropped you off."

It was only ten o'clock. "You must have left early this morning. Everything okay?"

"Yeah. We just needed some space."

"Really?"

"No. We had a fight."

"I'm sorry. Are you at home now?"

"Yeah."

89

"Give me fifteen minutes to call home—if I don't, Mom and Dad will be on the phone to the governor, asking him to send out search and rescue teams for me—then come on over."

Chapter 17

I hung up with Abbie, called home, and listened while Mom and Dad got settled at the kitchen table.

"I'm sorry we weren't here Tuesday evening to take your call," said Mom. "Thank you for the text message. That was very nice of that boy to clean up your car."

"Yes, it was, Mom. He restored my faith in the school. Of course, Lionel had already told me he hasn't had any problems with racism on campus and he's been here three years."

"Why would he have any problems?"

"I guess I didn't mention. Lionel is black."

"I see. It's good to know he feels safe there. Have you been seeing him?"

"Yes, as a matter of fact. We made a trip to Yellow Springs yesterday."

"What's that?"

"A little town west of here. They have a historic college."

"I'm so glad to hear you're having fun on the weekends. You don't want to get burned out."

"Not at all. In fact, I'm getting some help on my research from the chairman of the history department. He's written books on the history of the college and the religious commune that started it, and he's really interested in what I'm finding out about the mural."

"Are you supposed to report to him about it?"

"No. He's helping me with the history behind the mural. That saves me some time. It makes my job easier. He's like a mentor for my research."

"That's wonderful."

Dad spoke up. "Have you taken a good look at the car? In direct sunlight? You have to bend down and look at it from every angle."

"Yep, all good, Dad."

"Did my check arrive?"

"Not yet. Do you want me to send it back or tear it up?"

"No, you cash that check and set the money aside. That will be your rainy-day fund."

Ordinarily I would have refused, or at least argued, but the end of the month was approaching and I was already bumming rides so I wouldn't have to burn gas when I needed to go into Blanton for supplies. "Thanks, Dad. I'll do that."

"Nicole, honey, the funniest thing happened."

Whenever Mom described an event as "the funniest thing," she meant to suggest it was unexpected when in fact it was the result of her determined effort.

"What's that, Mom?"

"I ran into Mrs. Petretti at Albertson's."

Crossing paths at the supermarket with any given neighbor from our block was practically guaranteed to happen once a month.

Mom continued. "She said Anna is back home. You remember their daughter, Anna?"

Anna was a year younger than me and we had attended the same schools, so of course I remembered her. "Yes, Mom. Do you mean she's back in town or she's living in their house?"

"Back in town. She got an apartment with some other girls. It turns out she didn't like Seattle all that much. She's working at one of those fancy restaurants downtown, but she still does her music. She gets together with friends, and they play at festivals and different places."

"Wow! That's just like what you want me to do. What a coincidence that you should run into Mrs. Petretti this week!"

"She was just there at the supermarket. Anyway, do you have Anna's number? You should give her a call."

"Yeah, I have it, Mom. Thanks."

"Have the police found out any more about your student?" asked Dad. "The one who was killed?"

"Nothing definite, Dad. The county sheriff came by to talk to me about one of my other students, and he said it's now a criminal investigation, so I guess they don't think it's an accident."

"Do you mean she may have been killed deliberately?"

I decided Mom and Dad didn't need to know about Devon and his high school girlfriend. "I don't know, Dad. The sheriff wasn't giving out any information."

"Wait a minute," said Mom. "Are you saying she might have been murdered?"

"Yes, that is possible."

"Oh, my god! Nicole! I don't think you should be living there."

"Mom, people get murdered in San Francisco too."

"Yes, but this is a big city."

"So what? That doesn't mean I'd be any safer there."

"But it's . . . it's just different. I don't know. You talk to her, Terry."

"Nicole, darlin', just keep us informed. Let us know what this sheriff has to say."

"I will, Dad."

"Call us or send us a message. We're always here for you."

"I know, Dad. I'll be fine, Mom. Bye."

I knew Mom and Dad were in for an intense conversation about letting me be independent without letting me do anything too dangerous. I'd taken part in that conversation several times in the past. I also knew that in San Francisco I would be no safer than I was in this rural corner of Ohio, but that we would all worry less, because the risks were familiar. It wasn't going to be a peaceful morning for them or for me.

I put on the kettle, turned on the oven in my all-in-one kitchen, and changed into jeans and a sweater. The teapot was on the table steeping when Abbie arrived looking tired and stressed. Her shoulders were rounded and her blonde hair looked like she had combed it with her fingers. I got out the dough I had mixed earlier for almond cookies.

"Was it a bad fight?" I asked.

She settled at the cafe table. "No. I don't know."

"It's too bad you have to miss spending the day with her."

"I guess."

She sat looking out the window while I rolled out the dough and put the cookies on a sheet. One advantage of having a tiny range was that the oven took very little time to heat up. I put the cookies in, set the timer for ten minutes, and sat down across from her. "You look really sad."

Abbie shook her head. "I don't know what to do. It's our situation. We don't see each other all week, and when the weekend comes, we each have an agenda. She wants to talk about her work; I want to talk about my work. She wants to stay in; I want to go out. We end up arguing about everything: what movie to see, whether to get take out or cook. It's crazy."

"It's too bad you can't live together."

She laughed, but it was bitter. "Sure. I could publish a significant book, a job could open up at Pitt or Carnegie Mellon, and I could beat out the three hundred other applicants. It should only take about ten years for those planets to line up."

I poured tea for both of us.

She stared out the window again. When she spoke, her voice was heavy with irony. "Or Chillicothe could suddenly rival Pittsburgh as a financial center, and she could get a job down here as an analyst. Or we could break up and I could take my pick of all the single lesbians on the faculty. No, wait, I forgot: There aren't any."

"When you put it like that, it sounds hopeless."

She faced me. "Sorry, Nicole. I just clouded up and rained all over your Sunday morning."

The timer went off. I got the cookies out of the oven and

put them on a plate. "Here, these will bring you good

She bit into one. "Mmm! Worth eating even wi... good luck. How are things with Lionel?"

"We went to Yellow Springs yesterday."

Abbie stared at me with smirk on her face. "And?"

"We had a good time."

She chuckled. "Are you going to make me beg for details?"

"As we were on our way there, we talked about the president's speech at convocation. Lionel thinks the change to emphasizing career preparation is more serious than the name change."

"He's right about that."

"Then we walked around Antioch's campus, and he said they're re-emphasizing liberal arts. They can do that because that's been their tradition since the place was founded, therefore the alumni will support it."

She nodded. "That's an interesting point. I'm not sure where that leaves us."

"We couldn't figure that out either. He mentioned Jacob is working on a biography of Fuchs. Of course, the business school will be operating before it's published."

Abbie was staring at me again, and the smirk was back. "What else?"

I didn't know what to say.

She leaned across the table toward me. "You drove to Yellow Springs and back, had wonderful collegial conversations all the way, and . . . ? Did you finish off the day with a bang, so to speak?"

I didn't quite get my napkin up fast enough to catch the spray of cookie crumbs that exploded from between my lips. Abbie pounded on my back to make sure I wasn't choking, and we sat back and laughed like a pair of lunatics.

Once I caught my breath, I said, "Let me be clear about that. It's not on the menu."

"Oh, Nicole! Tsk, tsk, tsk. We're not getting any

younger."

"Don't remind me."

I poured more tea and we ate the last of the cookies.

Abbie looked serious. "You said on the phone you crossed paths with a student this morning, and it was a little scary."

"Devon. Kate's boyfriend."

"The one who beat up his girlfriend in high school?"

I frowned at her. "The one who was accused of doing that. Let's not jump to conclusions. The sheriff questioned him about it, and he thought I had told the sheriff. We straightened it out."

"Straightened it out how?"

"I made it clear I didn't tell the sheriff anything he didn't already know."

"So why is he stalking you on a Sunday morning?"

"He wasn't stalking me. We just happened to cross paths. Stop trying to turn this into something it wasn't."

"Nicole, you have to be careful. Don't go out running alone."

"Do you want to run with me?"

The way Abbie looked at me suggested she was considering a mental health intervention. "I'll walk you to the gym and you can use a treadmill," she said.

"I will if you will."

"You feed me cookies, and now you're telling me I need to lose weight?"

"No. I just hate treadmills. You may as well be on a hamster wheel."

Abbie stood up and stretched. "Just don't take chances like that anymore. If something happens to you, there won't be anyone around to help me feel sorry for myself. Thanks for the snack."

"Before you go, I want to ask you about something."

Chapter 18

Abbie stood by the door, awaiting my question. "Do you remember last week I told you about Devon being accused of assaulting his girlfriend?"

"Sure."

"I wanted to find out from her if that's true, so I found her on Budstem, and she agreed to be my buddy because a couple of my students are friends of hers from high school."

Abbie started looking skeptical.

I went on. "This morning I sent her an email saying I'd like to interview her for my show on NPR."

She looked very skeptical. "Your show on NPR?"

"I lied."

"Why would you lie to her?"

"So she'll agree to meet with me. Once I'm with her, I can ask her about this incident with Devon when they were in high school."

Abbie took a breath and let it out slowly. "And what is it you want to ask me about?"

"Assuming she agrees to meet with me, I'll have to get myself to Ohio Northern University next Saturday morning. It's in Ada, a small town near Lima, about a three-hour drive."

"So . . . ?"

"I've never taken a long car trip like that. Before I moved here, I didn't even have a driver's license because I never needed to drive in San Francisco. The farthest I've ever driven was down here from Columbus when I picked up the car from the dealer last month. Is there anything special I need to do before going on a six-hour round trip?"

"Are you up to date on oil changes?"

"I think the dealer was supposed to take care of that."

"What about other scheduled maintenance?"

"I don't know. Where do I get the schedule?"

"It's in the owner's manual."

"Does that come with the car?"

Abbie laughed. "We'd better take my car and leave early."

"Aren't you going to Pittsburgh next weekend?"

"I seriously doubt it."

"I'm sorry to hear that, but I'll be glad to have your company."

"It'll be better for me than hanging out here by myself. I'll see you later. Those quizzes aren't going to grade themselves."

I managed to come up with a handout for my art history class and gave it to them Monday morning. It told them the purpose of the assignment, specified the length of the paper, defined thesis statement, evidence, and conclusion, gave examples of each, listed the dates when class would meet in the chapel, and ended with a brief bibliography. This was like giving coloring books to students in a drawing class.

Ursula Wilmot pulled a hole-punch from her backpack, punched the necessary three holes in my assignment sheet, added a reinforcement around each hole, and clipped the sheet into her binder behind the appropriate index tab. I'm all for keeping things tidy, but she could have done it after class.

Back in my office, while lunching on a cheese sandwich and tea from my thermos, I thought about my situation. Through all those years of college and graduate school, I poured my heart and soul into becoming a scholar, but I didn't learn to be a teacher.

Not that I couldn't teach. Give me a room full of students like Kate, and I could take them on a journey of discovery through the world of art. But, faced with a room full of students with differing abilities, diverse attitudes about learning, and contrary reasons for going to college, I didn't know where to start.

I wanted to continue teaching as I had on that first day when I met my class in the chapel, showing them how to observe, how to research, and how to write about their discoveries. But with Kate gone, there was no one in class to set the standard, to prove to the others that the work can be done by people just like themselves.

Surely I was not the first assistant professor to go through this in her first semester of teaching. Others must have struggled with the same problem. Abbie had started her teaching career only three years earlier. I could ask her.

Byron Hawley appeared in my doorway, waving the handout. "Thanks for this," he said.

"You're welcome," I replied.

He sat in the chair beside my desk, and ran his eyes over the page. "This looks very interesting. Looks like a lot of work. It's clear, though. I see what you're getting at."

I wished I could say the same for his mumblings. "Do you have any questions about the assignment, Byron?"

He pursed his lips and hummed. "I'll probably need some help with this."

"I'll be glad to help you. Does anything come to mind as a topic?"

"Mmm. Not yet. I'll have to think about it."

"All right. Look over your notes and the sketch you did when we met in the chapel. You could think about it this way: Are you more interested in the artist's technique or in his subject?"

He chewed on that for a moment. "I see what you mean. I'll do that and get back to you. I just wanted to stop by and make sure we have an understanding that I will need some help on this."

"That's what I'm here for," I replied.

He grinned. "Good. Thanks."

He left and I could only wonder why he thought we needed to reach understanding that I would help a student with the paper I assigned.

Tuesday and Thursday were my days to breathe easy at lunchtime because I had the afternoons free for preparing classes, grading, and getting back to my research. All of that was delayed on this Tuesday by a meeting of the art department.

The four of us settled around a table in one of the seminar rooms in the Arts and Humanities Building. I unpacked my lunch of fruit, yogurt and rye toast. Wilma Halberstadt had a sandwich from the snack bar in the Student Center. Irving Zorn had brought a pizza in a cardboard box, the "meat-lover's special." Within moments, the room reeked of garlic and pork sausage. Frank was keeping it old school with a PB&J and an apple.

"Career preparation. Great opportunity," said Frank, opening the meeting. "On board with this. Real game changer for the school and for us. Ideas?"

Halberstadt, our specialist in art education, was the first to speak. "Well, of course, we have been preparing students for careers in teaching all along." When she said, "we," she meant, "I," but it was nice of her to take the rest of us along for the ride.

"Emphasis on that," said Frank. "Other ideas?"

Zorn was preoccupied with his pizza, so I decided to put my oar in the water. "I'm a little unclear on whether this means we emphasize careers in art history or that we show how art history is relevant to lots of careers."

"Excellent thinking," cried Frank. Apparently, he missed the gist of my remark, which was that I didn't know what to think.

Halberstadt turned to me and said, in a tone that did not invite discussion, "It means careers in art history."

"Nothing wrong with that." Frank paused to wash down

the last of his sandwich. "For my own part, painters. Since the Greeks. Lascaux. Prehistoric. Basic human impulse. Still relevant. Several alumni with promising careers."

I decided to try again. "I see what you mean, Frank, but I'm also thinking that a lot of students have taken your painting classes over the years, and they might be willing to write letters saying how things they learned from you are relevant to whatever career they chose."

Halberstadt rolled her eyes and checked her watch.

"Absolutely." Frank nodded. "Alumni, as I was saying."

"Frank, I mean not just the ones who have careers as painters, the others as well."

"Of course. Contact them all."

He turned and looked at Zorn, who had eaten the last of his pizza and announced his accomplishment with a partly stifled belch.

Zorn saw that we were all looking his way and took a moment to gather his energy. "Career. What does that mean? We do things for money, sure. But what about vocation? What about the things we do for love? That's the original meaning of 'amateur.' The word has a negative connotation these days, but it didn't always. So, I'm a little unclear on all this. I think the president needs to be more specific."

Coming from a painter who collected nice sums of money turning out abstract canvases beloved by interior designers, this was ironic to say the least.

Frank was nodding. "More to come. Just the beginning. Get our ideas out there. Your best thinking in writing. On my desk next week."

Halberstadt was already halfway out of her chair when he finished speaking. Zorn was right behind her.

As I stacked my food containers, Frank asked me, "Good semester so far?"

This didn't seem like a moment to talk about Kate, so I put on a happy face and said, "I think so."

"Teaching the mural. Wonderful idea. Very creative."

"Thank you. The students have responded very well to it. Bringing them face to face with a real work of art means so much more than showing them slides, which are only pictures of art works."

He nodded. "So true."

"My problem is, there aren't any other works of art on campus except for a painting here and there in someone's office. I'm not sure what I can do for an encore."

"Hmm. Good point," said Frank, squinting at the far wall.

"I wish I could put them all on a bus and take them to the Columbus Museum of Art for a day."

"Worthwhile. Yes."

"Is there funding for that kind of a trip?"

"Possibly."

"If so, I'd like to make plans so I can build on our momentum."

"Scheduling problems, of course."

"That's true. They would have to miss their other classes."

"Still, good thinking. We'll talk more."

I walked back to my Rabbit Hutch to pick up my art-historian tools. Along the way, I thought about careers related to art history. Museums have curators, but those jobs are scarce, and the pay is low. People who own and work in galleries have to know some art history, but they have to know more about sales and marketing. Of course, there's always teaching, but teaching teachers to teach teachers is in the end a Ponzi scheme. The best justification for art history is that people have communicated with pictures as long as there have been people. To ignore the medium is to ignore a large portion of human experience.

Under the circumstances, my best strategy was to write a memo about careers in museums, galleries, and schools, and then to start my own research on alumni in other fields. If I started right away, I might come up with something in time to make a difference.

It felt good to lock myself away in the chapel for the afternoon. I needed time to exercise my mind by doing the work I had shared with Kate.

Chapter 19

I resumed my study of the mural by searching the crown of the tree for other clusters of coffins and found several, as I had expected I would. On a new page in my sketchbook I drew a rough outline of the crown of the tree, mapped the location of each cluster, and numbered them. There were seven.

I looked at the cluster I had discovered on Thursday and confirmed what I had seen: five coffins, three containing men, two containing women. On a fresh page in my notebook, I wrote "Coffin Clusters" at the top, and below it, "1. Three men, two women." Nothing else to say, really.

Clusters number two and three were essentially the same, with two men and two women, and four men and three women, respectively. I recorded them too on the "Coffin Clusters" page.

In cluster number four I found something different. It had four men and two women, and one of the women had a smile on her face. Why had the muralist given this one corpse a personality? Maybe she was the muralist's wife. Maybe she had some special function in the community. It crossed my mind that she might have been happy to die, but that seemed too macabre.

On a hunch, I scanned the scenes in the middle row of the wall. There was no Smiling Woman among the congregation outside the church, but I found her singing in the choir. The hymnbook she held covered half her face so only half her smile was visible. It was easy to overlook, but once spotted it was unmistakable. I also found her in the cooking scene in the bottom row, cradling a mixing bowl in one arm. Her head was turned to the side so her face was seen in profile, but the little bit of her mouth that was visible turned upward. I felt my blood pumping as I recorded all this in my notebook.

In cluster number five, with one man and three women, I found another individual. This man had several parallel lines drawn on either side of his head and no ears visible. This seemed like a simple way of indicating long hair. I looked for him elsewhere in the mural and didn't find him, but in the process I found another recognizable individual, Smiling Man, in the orchard.

By this time, the afternoon light was dimmer, and my eyes were starting to ache from looking through the binoculars, drawing, and taking notes. I was happy to quit for the day because I had new information to ponder. Apparently, the muralist had had more in mind than depicting the life of the community and identifying Felix Fuchs as the leader. He had also identified three others: Smiling Woman, Mr. Longhair, and Smiling Man. I needed to find out who they were and why they were important enough to be identified in the mural.

I still didn't know what Kate meant when she wrote on the day she died that she had "some good ideas about what one of the coffins in the mural might mean." I now had questions about what several of the coffins might mean, but I couldn't imagine which one she had in mind. Still I was encouraged. Doing the work felt good. I felt closer to Kate for having worked through the images she had studied during her last days. And I still had two clusters to go. One of them might contain a coffin that had a singular interest.

Although I couldn't read the archived documents of the commune, I could skim back through Jacob's book, *Tree of Life*, and see if there were an especially cheerful woman and man in the history of the commune, or if there was a man who was opposed to haircuts. If all else failed, I could take it up with Jacob. Though he hadn't come up with a good theory about why there were coffins in the treetop, he might know something about these individuals I had discovered.

Sheriff Adams called Tuesday evening and asked to meet me in my office the next day at three, but would not say why, which irritated me. When he arrived Wednesday afternoon, I was at my desk, grading quizzes.

He sat in the chair next to my desk and took out his notebook. "I understand you had an altercation with Devon Manus on Sunday morning."

He caught me off-guard with that one. "I wouldn't call it an altercation."

"Would you mind telling me about it?"

"Wait a minute. How do you know about this? Did someone call you?"

"I'm on campus to pick up Devon Manus and take him in for questioning. When I called campus security to ask for their cooperation, the officer I spoke to mentioned you had required assistance."

"What do you mean 'take him in?'"

"We're not arresting him just yet, although we may seek to hold him overnight. Now, would you tell me what happened?"

"I ran into him on campus Sunday morning. He was pretty upset with me."

"Do you recall what he said?"

"He thought I had told you about the incident with his high school girlfriend. I told him I only confirmed what you already knew. I also told him he probably had an alibi since he was at Marten's for an hour after Kate left."

"Well that's no longer the case." I tried to read the sheriff's face, but his expression was as wooden as ever. "The medical examiner was pretty clear. The victim could not have died before midnight."

I covered my mouth with both hands. It felt like

something actors do to show they're shocked, but I didn't care. I wanted to cover part of my face and not let him see everything I was feeling: the loss of Kate, outrage at a life cut short, and more. When I had caught my breath, I said, "First of all, you mean 'Kate Conrad,' not 'the victim.'"

If the sheriff was surprised by my remark, he didn't show it. "Yes, ma'am."

"Second, Devon drove his friends back to campus before eleven thirty, so that leaves him in the clear."

"But he would have had time to return to the scene."

"How?" I asked. "He couldn't know she would be walking back to campus. She might have gotten a ride back with someone else. He wouldn't drive around in the middle of the night hoping to see her by chance."

"We're looking into all those possibilities."

"Doesn't he live in a dorm? What about his roommate?"

"His roommate went home for the weekend."

"But there would be other people on the floor where he lives."

"No one remembers seeing him in the dorm after midnight."

"He probably just went to bed when he got back at eleven thirty."

The sheriff nodded. "We're looking into all possibilities."

I hugged myself to avoid shivering.

"Dr. Noonan, you seem convinced that Devon Manus did not kill Kate Conrad. Why is that?"

"I don't see why he would."

Adams looked out the window and took a moment to think about that. "You said they quarreled. He doesn't deny it. A young man gets his feelings hurt when a woman turns away from him. And he has a history."

"A history?"

"The incident with his girlfriend during his senior year in high school."

"Is that confirmed?"

"We're looking into that."

"He was never arrested. There were no charges. He said the local police, his parents, and her parents all agreed to keep it quiet. What does the girl say?"

The sheriff's already stern expression hardened a few more degrees. "I don't think we need to involve her and her family."

"I'm just asking whether or not you talked to the girlfriend."

"Dr. Noonan, I understand you are concerned about your student. I told you before: I am approaching this with an open mind, and he will be treated fairly. Now, if you'll excuse me, my deputy is waiting."

He stood up and left.

I closed my office door, picked up the largest book I could find—a collection of full-color reproductions of Renaissance masterpieces—and slammed it down on my desk. It made a satisfying bang followed by a reverberation.

He patronized me. He may as well have patted me on the head when he said he understood I was concerned about my student.

He sounded so confident when he said, "He has a history," yet he had gotten his version of Devon's history from the police in Mansfield, Devon's hometown, and I knew from my conversation with Devon they had nothing on record. So, really, all the sheriff had was hearsay.

And why in the world had he said, "I don't think we need to involve her and her family." There was something fishy about the way everyone was keeping this quiet.

Chapter 20

Feeling more determined than ever to find out directly from Teresa Zannetti whether Devon had assaulted her, I opened my personal email account and checked the inbox. Teresa still had not replied to my invitation to meet. It was possible she had looked for my name on the NPR website and hadn't found it. Or she might have checked with her high-school friends in my art appreciation class and found out I was a professor of art history, not a radio producer. The more I thought of it, the sillier my strategy seemed, but I thought I might as well give it a few more days while I tried to think of another approach.

Back at my Rabbit Hutch Wednesday evening, I stir fried some veggies and tofu and treated myself to a glass of wine and an old movie, *Crouching Tiger, Hidden Dragon*. While cleaning up the dishes, I recalled the way I turned down Lionel's invitation to have a glass of wine in his home after our trip to Yellow Springs. Somehow I felt as if I should make it up to him.

I did some research online and discovered we had not exhausted all that southern Ohio had to offer. We hadn't even touched Cincinnati. After jotting down information about several attractions, although it was late, I gave Dr. Lionel Bell a call.

When he answered, "Hi Nicole," his voice sounded surprised and delighted.

"Good evening, Lionel. Have you ever taken the Underground Tour of Cincinnati?"

"I can't say I have. Why?"

"I was just thinking that an afternoon tour could be followed by dinner at Moerlein Lager House."

"Well, that sounds delightful," he said. "Are we talking about this coming weekend?"

"That's right."

He sighed. "The only problem is I'm going away this weekend, and I probably won't be back until Monday evening."

"Where are you going?"

"Home. New York. Mom needs help while Dad is recovering from surgery."

My mood fell. "That's wonderful that you can be there for them. I hope your father gets well quickly."

"Shouldn't be a problem. He just needs some time. Can I take a rain check on that trip to Cincinnati?"

"Of course." I did my best to sound casual and unconcerned. "Maybe next week or the week after. Just let me know."

"I'm putting it on my calendar for next week. I'll be in touch when I get back."

"Sounds good, Lionel. Have a safe trip."

I was disappointed by the postponement, but glad we were on the calendar. I would check in with him next week to see how his father was doing and to reignite anticipation of our next trip.

At noon on Thursday, I went to the snack bar, picked up a sandwich, and hurried over to the chapel. While I ate, I prepared questions for the students in my art history class so they would know what to look for when we met to look at the mural tomorrow morning. Teaching this way felt like organizing an Easter-egg hunt.

Once I had my questions written, I got back to studying

the mural, picking up where I left off with cluster number six. It had five coffins. Four of them were occupied by women, and one of them by a man. The man was easily identifiable by his long nose: Felix Fuchs. Apparently, the muralist had painted a miniature biography of the founder: preaching to his followers in Germany, working as part of the community in the fields and orchards, and buried alongside women who may have represented a wife and sisters or other relatives. Similarly, the muralist had painted biographies of Smiling Woman, singing in the choir, cooking with the other women, and buried with her family in cluster number four, as well as Mr. Longhair, building, harvesting, and buried with his family in cluster number five.

Based on this pattern, I expected to find Smiling Man in cluster number seven, but I didn't. Instead I found smaller coffins with children inside them as indicated by short pants for the boys and sack dresses for the girls. There were eight of them. One of the girls had a long nose. One of the boys had long hair. Apparently, Fuchs and Mr. Longhair had each lost a child. The six other children were anonymous although one had spots all over him. The spots were too few and too large to represent a disease such as measles, and they were visible not only on his face, hands, and bare legs, but also on his pants and shirt. I couldn't guess what they might mean.

This stage in a research project is like reaching a place on a mountain trail where a gap in the trees lets you see the floor of the valley from which you ascended and the side of the mountain you still have to climb. The climber is both rewarded for all her effort and challenged by what lies ahead. I felt exhilarated by all I knew about the mural and daunted by all the things I still did not understand.

I now knew that, along with giving an overview of life in the Eden Commune, the muralist had recorded the lives and deaths of Fuchs, Smiling Woman, and Mr. Longhair, plus the deaths of two of their children. He had also recorded the life of Smiling Man. Except for Fuchs, I did not know who these individuals were, and I did not understand what made them worth noting among the many other anonymous people of the commune. My review of Jacob's book, *Tree of Life,* had turned up no clues as to their identities.

I pulled out my phone, opened my email, and found Kate's message, sent the day she died. "In the library today, I found some art history books that gave me some good ideas about what one of the coffins in the mural might mean." Which coffin was she talking about? If I had to pick one, it would be the one with the spotted child because it was least like any of the others.

For a moment, I wished I could ask the college librarians what books Kate checked out and what online searches she made on that Friday afternoon before she died, but of course that was impossible, and for good reason. In order to protect freedom of speech, the librarian's code of ethics holds research done by library patrons confidential. That's an important rule, but this one time I would have loved to have an exception.

Kate probably had notes about the mural in the notebook she kept for class, but looking at it would mean asking her parents for access to her personal possessions. Although I didn't like the idea of intruding on their grief, perhaps the condolence card I had sent after she died would assure them of my good intentions. They might also appreciate my wish to continue her research and ultimately to give her the footnote she deserved. Since the notebook looked like the only way of being sure which coffin Kate had been interested in, I would have to call them.

On Friday morning I was relieved to find an email from Teresa Zannetti in my inbox. She said she would like to be a guest on my radio show and suggested we meet at a cafe across the street from the Ohio Northern University campus. I felt a twinge of guilt but told myself it was for a greater good.

I sent Abbie a text suggesting we leave early the next morning.

In art history class, I passed out a sheet with the questions I had written Thursday afternoon while studying the mural. The students were thrilled. As I read the questions aloud and commented on them, the students all started jotting answers beneath each one and showing their sheets to each other when they thought I wasn't looking. Ursula Wilmot was more pleased than anyone, but she kept her answers to herself. This wasn't my favorite way to teach, but it was getting us through the semester.

Back in my office, I called the registrar, and asked for Kate Conrad's home phone number and her parents' names. Once I had them, I focused for a moment on my wish that this call would bring some comfort to the Conrads and dialed. Kate's mother answered, and I said, "Mrs. Conrad, my name is Nicole Noonan. I am a professor of art history at Fuchs College."

"Yes?"

She sounded hopeful. I forged ahead. "Kate was in my art history class."

"Yes. She loved that class. She told us all about it."

"She was a wonderful student. Very imaginative. She contributed so many wonderful ideas to our class discussions."

Mrs. Conrad was getting choked up. "Thank you, Dr. Noonan. I am glad to hear that. It helps to know she was happy."

"She was. And it was a pleasure and an honor to teach her."

"Thank you. I'll tell her father when he gets home. It's so nice of you to take time to call. I'm sure you have so many students to see."

"That's all right, Mrs. Conrad. If you have a moment, I wonder if I could ask you about something."

"Of course."

This felt like crossing a creek by walking on a falling log. "Kate sent me an email saying she had an idea for her term paper, and that she hoped it would be worth a footnote in my research. You see, I explained to the class that when scholars mention someone else's idea, they recognize it in a footnote. So, I would like to include her idea in my work and mention her name. It would be a way of remembering the work she did in art history."

"I know she would have loved that."

"The problem is, we never had a chance to discuss her idea. So, I need to look at her notebook for art history class. If you like, I can visit this weekend and look through it if that wouldn't inconvenience you."

"You won't need to do that. We mailed it to another professor at the college last week, Dr. Schumacher. He called and said he needed to see it. I guess she talked about her work with him too. Does he also teach art history?"

I could feel my pulse throbbing in my neck. "No, he's in the history department, but I know he was helping her." It took everything I had to keep my voice pleasant and reassuring.

"Well, maybe you could get it from him."

"I will do that, Mrs. Conrad. Thank you so much. I am sorry for your loss."

"Thank you, Dr. Noonan. It really helps to know she was doing well in school and happy. Goodbye."

I hung up and headed for the stairwell. My heart was galloping, and when it does that I find it's best to trot up and down a few flights of stairs to burn off the adrenaline so I can think clearly.

Chapter 21

Once I had stabilized, I went back to my office and thought about what I had just learned. Mrs. Conrad said they sent the notebook to Jacob last week. Yet, when I talked to him in the chapel last Thursday—over a week ago—he acted as if he were unaware that there were coffins in the mural or that Kate was studying them. Obviously he went behind my back to find out what Kate was doing in my course.

I began to suspect he intended to use Kate's idea as his own, though I hated to think that a colleague would plagiarize the work of a student. I had thought of him as a mentor. He seemed so eager to help when I visited his office and asked about the mural in. During our sessions in the chapel, he showed such enthusiasm for the ideas we shared. But apparently he'd been spying on me the whole time.

I could confront him and demand to see Kate's notebook, but he would surely deny he had it. Then what? I couldn't ask Kate's parents to tell the dean they sent the notebook to him. It would be cruel to involve them in a faculty spat when they were grieving. I wasn't aware of any rules or customs that apply to the intellectual property of a deceased student. Even if there were some formal way to complain about what he was doing, I wouldn't stand a chance against the guy who had literally written the book about the history of the place, had been on the faculty for more than thirty years, and whose family was here when the community was founded.

Perhaps I could bypass Jacob and figure out what Kate had discovered without access to her notebook. I had worked with Kate and had some idea of how she thought. Recalling my most recent visit to the mural, I had a strong feeling that the coffin with the spotted child was the one she had in mind. I could do my own research on the culture of the region and form some idea of what that image might mean. I could also talk to Lionel about it when he was back from New York since he proved on our trip to Yellow Springs he was well read on local history. All that sounded like a lot of work, and most of it might be skipped if I could get my hands on that notebook, but I could no longer trust Jacob.

Instead, after replicating Kate's discovery, I could let the campus know what she had done by teaching it to my art history class, and perhaps by inviting the student newspaper to write an article about it. If I let the whole campus know Kate discovered the coffins and the spotted child, he wouldn't dare put the discovery in a scholarly journal as it if were his own. In effect, I would stop his plagiarism by simply doing my job.

The sooner I worked out the meaning of the spotted child, the better

On Saturday morning, I got up before sunrise to make a thermos of tea and pack up the muffins I had made Friday evening. Abbie picked me up and we hit the road just after dawn. Once we were past Chillicothe, I broke out the tea and muffins and we had our breakfast as we cruised up Route 35 toward Dayton. The scenery was familiar from last weekend's trip with Lionel.

"Explain something to me," said Abbie. "Assuming this young woman doesn't get up and leave when you reveal you are not in fact a radio producer, she will either tell you that this guy . . . your student . . ."

"Devon."

"Right. Devon either did beat her up when they were in high school or he didn't. So, you'll know one way or the other. Then what?"

"Well, if he did, then it's more likely he killed Kate, and

I'll be glad the sheriff is investigating him. But if Devon didn't hurt Teresa, I want to make sure the sheriff knows that."

"And—just remind me—why wouldn't the sheriff know that?"

"He was evasive when I asked him whether he talked to this girl."

"So we're driving three hours up to Ada, Ohio to make sure the sheriff is doing his job?" Abbie raised an eyebrow.

"I know it's a lot to ask."

"No. Like I said, it beats staring at four walls."

Ohio farm country looked different from California farm country, cute by comparison. In the Central Valley of California crops are raised on a vast, industrial scale. Even around Salinas where the crops require lots of labor, the flat fields seem to go on forever. But in Ohio it seemed one could always see the road or the line of trees that bordered the farm, and the land seemed to have shoulders. The road pitched and rolled and curved, making for a more entertaining ride.

"Since we have a couple of hours to kill," I said, "what was your first semester like?"

"How do you mean?"

"Were you comfortable teaching your classes?"

"I wouldn't say comfortable. I got through it."

"Did you feel like you knew how to teach?"

"Oh God, no."

That was a relief. "So what did you do?"

"Just kept at it. I'd see a story in the news that related to some concept in my course, so I'd copy it and throw it in my file for next time. I tried to get them to think about something in their world and then show them it's something economists have already thought about."

"I like that. In effect, you illustrated the textbook with current events."

"Right."

"So then for the assignment or for the exam, did you ask them to solve a problem in economics or just to recognize the material you've covered?"

"I have yet to meet the student who wants to think like an economist, let alone be one. My situation is a little different. Nobody takes 'macroeconomics' for fun. They take it because it will help them get ahead in the business world. So I help them understand what economists are talking about."

"But that's not how you think about economics."

"No, but, as I said, my students aren't going to become economists."

"Mine aren't going to become art historians either. Thanks, Abbie. That gives me some things to think about."

"I thought your history class was going great since you started them on the mural."

"It was. So long as I had Kate in class, showing them how to think like art historians made sense. With her gone, I'm the only one in the room who wants to do that."

Abbie stared through the windshield for a few moments. "We spend years in grad school surrounded by people who are scholars, and then we get a job teaching people who are not going to be scholars. It's a shock. We have to find out what our subject has to offer to people who are going to be managers, entrepreneurs, paralegals, tradesmen, and so on. Don't worry about it Noonan. You're doing fine and you'll get better."

We pulled into Ada a little after nine thirty. The streets were busy in anticipation of that afternoon's football game on the campus. I guessed folks turned out in force for home games at Ohio Northern because there didn't seem to be much else in town to attract a crowd.

We parked a few streets away from campus and took a walk to wake ourselves up after the three-hour drive. What we could see of the campus from Main Street was fairly impressive. At about ten minutes before ten, we moved the car into the parking lot in front of the Northern on Main Cafe. I went in first and got a small table. Abbie came in a minute later and sat at the counter. It was comforting to look across the room and see her sitting tall at on a stool, blonde hair caught in the morning light.

I asked for coffee and two menus and divided my time between watching the door and choosing an omelet. At ten on the dot a young lady walked in and stopped to look around the room. She was, I guessed, a little taller than me, dressed business casual with navy slacks and a pink sweater over a white blouse. I wasn't immediately sure if she was Teresa Zannetti, because she had her hair pulled back. She had no such trouble recognizing me. She would have seen my photo on Budstem.

Chapter 22

Teresa Zannetti sat opposite me with a big smile on her face and took a CD out of her purse and set it on the table. She must have brought samples of her radio shows. I lost my appetite at the thought of how I had raised her expectations of a career breakthrough, and was about to turn her day around and send it in a much less pleasant direction.

"Order whatever you want," I said. "It's on me."

"I'll just have some coffee."

The waitress took our order.

I paused for a moment before saying, "Devon Manus is in serious trouble."

Her face froze for a few seconds. "Devon? What . . . ? Wait. Who are you?"

"I am the person who reached you on Budstem, Nicole Noonan, assistant professor of art history at Fuchs College."

She took a moment to let it sink in. "So you're not here about a show for NPR?"

"No. I lied. I needed to speak to you in person about Devon's situation, and I was afraid you wouldn't meet me. Devon is in sheriff's custody."

She gasped. "Why? What did he do?"

"I'm not sure he did anything. A student at Fuchs College was murdered two weeks ago, a young woman named Kate Conrad. She and Devon had been dating, but they were not out together the night she was killed."

"Why do they think he killed her?"

"The sheriff thinks Devon beat you up when the two of

you were dating in high school."

After she thought about that for a moment, her jaw dropped, and she said, "Oh my God!"

The waitress brought her coffee and my omelet and topped up my coffee cup while she was at it. I was glad for the distraction and took some time putting marmalade on my toast. Teresa needed time to understand what I had told her.

I took a bite of the omelet, followed by a bite of toast, and washed it down with coffee. "Did Sheriff Mason Adams of the Edwards County Sheriff's Department talk to you about this?"

She shook her head.

"Devon didn't hurt you, did he?"

She looked alarmed. "Why do you say that?"

"You're still sitting here with me."

She relaxed. "No. He didn't."

"Devon told me a man out jogging thought you were hurt and called the police, and after that everyone assumed Devon had hurt you. Is that what happened?"

A few tears escaped her eyes. She nodded. "I told them—the police, my parents, everybody—that he didn't do anything to me. I just slipped and fell, but they wouldn't believe me."

"Why not?"

She wrinkled her nose as if smelling something rotten. "It was all just a big mess. I don't know what happened."

"I don't know if the sheriff has brought charges against him yet, but Devon is very close to being arrested. It might help him if you called Sheriff Adams and told him what happened that night."

For the first time, she looked frightened. "I couldn't do that."

"It's important that they don't use this against him."

She kept her eyes down and shook her head. "No. No. I can't do that."

"Teresa . . ."

"No. I have to go." She put the CD back in her tote bag and picked up her jacket.

"Teresa, let me give you my card so you can get in touch with me."

She stood up. "No. And you didn't have to lie to me."

She turned and walked out.

I kept my eyes down, because I didn't want to know if people at the tables around me were staring.

The waitress came to the table. "Everything okay here? More coffee?"

"No, thanks. Just the check."

She walked away and Abbie slid into the seat where Teresa had sat. "How did it go?"

"Devon didn't hurt her, but she won't talk about it."

"Why not?

"She's scared."

"Of what?"

"I don't know."

Traffic streamed into Ada in advance of that afternoon's game, but it wasn't bad leaving town and getting on the freeway going south. We passed exit signs for roads and towns we had passed going the opposite direction about an hour ago. It felt like we were going in circles.

Meanwhile, inside me, my guts were twisting. I broke the silence. "That was not fun."

"Which part?"

"Playing a trick on a student."

"Well, Devon's not having much fun either."

"That's not her fault."

Abbie hummed for a few seconds as she thought about that. "It's a little bit her fault."

"How so?"

"She could speak up and clear him, but she won't."

"Yes, she could. So, why doesn't she?"

Abbie tapped her fingers on the steering wheel while she thought about it. "You said she seemed afraid, right?"

"Definitely. Deer in the headlights. She said, 'No. I can't

talk about that,' and it wasn't 'can't' as in, 'I don't feel up to it.' It was more like, 'I'm not allowed to.'"

"So who won't allow her to talk?"

"In her situation, most likely a parent."

Abbie checked her mirrors, changed lanes, and passed a pickup truck loaded with furniture. When we were again cruising in the right lane, she asked, "Why would her mom or dad want her to keep quiet about a mildly embarrassing incident that happened a few years ago in high school?"

"I can't imagine. It's not as if she got pregnant or arrested for drugs, at least so far as we know."

Abbie's finger tapping reached a climax, and she hit the steering wheel with the heel of her hand. "Maybe it's not about her."

"What do you mean?"

"Does your phone get a signal here?"

I fished it out of my purse and checked. "It does."

"You said she's from Mansfield?"

"Yes."

"See if you can find a website for the city of Mansfield."

I typed the name of the town into my phone's browser and searched. The town's website was the first hit. "Got it."

"Does it list the mayor and city council members—people like that?"

"There's a city directory."

"Do you see anyone named Zannetti?"

I did a quick scan. "Not on this page. Let me try a search." I typed "Zannetti" into the search box and hit enter. "Nope. That name is not on the city's website. What's your idea?"

"If her dad is in politics, he might be protecting his reputation, not Teresa's. The same would be true for her mom."

"I see what you mean. Let me check something else. Mansfield is the County Seat for Richland County." I went to the county's website, searched for "Zannetti," and saw a portrait of a middle-aged man in a conservative suit. "Here he is, Judge Thomas P. Zannetti. Court of Common Pleas."

"Could be her father, but he could also be an uncle. See if you can find some local news stories with both her name and his."

I searched, scanned the list of headlines that turned up, and read one of the stories. "Yep. She won an essay contest in high school. The end of the story says she is the daughter of Maureen and Thomas Zannetti."

Abbie nodded. "Okay. Now go back to the county's website. Are judges elected?"

"Yes. judges in Richland County are elected to six-year terms. What does all this tell us?"

Abbie held up her right hand, as if warning me to slow down. "Just thinking out loud here. Let's say he was running for office back when Teresa and Devon had their little snafu. Would he want the voters to see news stories about his daughter and her boyfriend picked up by the police in some park?"

"No. He would not."

"It wouldn't even matter why they were picked up or whether there were any charges. The words 'daughter' and 'police' in the same headline would put a dent in his political aspirations."

I saw where Abbie was going with this. "So he might have used his influence to keep the police quiet and keep the story from getting out."

Abbie nodded. "And he might have imposed a gag order, so to speak, on daughter Teresa."

"If you're right, he's in the middle of a six-year term. He's not facing re-election now, so why would she be afraid to talk?"

"He might have higher ambitions."

"I don't know, Abbie. It's hard to imagine voters getting very upset about something his daughter did years ago. Maybe at the time, yeah, but not now."

Abbie stared out the windshield at the farmland we were passing. "Maybe whatever influence he used to keep the incident quiet wasn't strictly legal. Or maybe it just looks a little too insider. An opponent could still make an issue of it. I don't know. I'm just guessing about all these details. My point is, Teresa may be afraid of daddy and what might happen to her if she jeopardizes his career."

"Okay. Assuming that's true, I wonder if I could sell her on the idea that she could have a private phone conversation with Sheriff Adams and that it wouldn't go any further."

Abbie nodded. "It's worth a try."

When I got home, I looked up Teresa's Budstem root and found we were no longer buddies and most of her information was now visible to friends only. Smart girl. I took some comfort in the idea that I had taught her that lesson, and perhaps saved her from getting truly scammed. I still had her email address, but it didn't seem worth the trouble to write. I recalled her grim look as she left the diner. She did not want to hear from me ever again.

I decided to work the problem from the other end, and called the number on Sheriff Adams' card. It went to voicemail, and I left a message saying I had some information for him.

Chapter 23

Sheriff Adams called back on Sunday morning and suggested we meet in my office around eleven. That left time for me to call home. I hoped to reassure Mom and Dad by reporting the good news and leaving out the bad stuff.

Once we were all on the line, I thanked Dad for his check, and told him I was keeping that money for emergencies.

"Glad to hear it, darlin'," he said. "Let me know if you need more."

"Okay, Dad."

"Nicole, honey, did you call Anna Petretti?"

"Gosh, Mom, it's been such a busy week. I didn't get around to that, but I'm really making progress on my study of this mural in the college's old chapel." I decided they didn't need to know about Jacob going behind my back to get my student's notebook.

"That's wonderful," said Dad. "They're lucky to have you there."

"Thanks. I think it could tell us a lot about the history of the school. I might write an article for a history journal in addition to one for an art journal."

"Are you seeing Lionel?" asked Mom.

"We were going to do something this weekend, but he had to go to New York. His father's having surgery."

"Oh. That's too bad."

Dad asked, "Did security ever come up with anything about the vandalism?"

"No, Dad, but thanks for reminding me. They were

supposed to call me back, but they haven't. I'll have to check."

"Well, if your boyfriend hasn't had any of that trouble, it may have been a one-time thing."

"Right, Dad. That's a good point, although he's not my boyfriend."

"Nicole, Honey, did they find out anything about your student, the one who died?"

I could have told them the sheriff was focusing on another of my students as a suspect, and I didn't see much reason to bring it up since I now knew he had no history as an abuser. "They're still looking into that, Mom. I haven't heard anything definite."

I tried a couple more times to bring up my research, and they encouraged me, but it was clear they were more concerned about my personal life and my safety. Perhaps they felt somewhat reassured, but my insides felt like a rubber band stretched to the breaking point. Filtering out things that would only upset them was more strain than I wanted to bear on a Sunday morning. Maybe I would sit down later in the day and lay it all out in an email.

Adams' patrol car was parked outside the Arts and Humanities Building when I got there. We didn't speak as we walked together up the stairs to my office on the third floor. Once we were seated, he took out his notebook. "You said you have some information for me."

"Devon Manus did not abuse Teresa Zannetti."

"How do you know this?"

"I asked her, and she told me."

Adams said nothing for a moment, but his face flushed. "Dr. Noonan, you have crossed a line. When you start questioning people who are involved in the case, you are interfering with my investigation."

"The last time we talked, you told me you didn't want to involve her and her family. So, I wasn't talking to someone involved in your investigation."

"Do not twist my words. You know exactly what I mean.

If I even suspect you have influenced what this young woman might have to say about Manus, I will charge you with obstruction. Do I make myself clear?"

"Perfectly."

Adams studied me for a moment. "If I have one of my deputies talk to Ms. Zannetti, will she confirm what you're saying?"

"Yes, but it would be best to make this confidential. I think she's under pressure not to talk about it, probably from her parents."

Adams shook his head slightly, the only physical sign of frustration he allowed himself.

"Sheriff, without this supposed history of abuse, it seems much less likely that Devon killed Kate."

"He still has no alibi for the time of the murder."

"He was in bed asleep. There's nothing suspicious about that."

"He had quarreled with the vic—with Ms. Conrad."

"Sheriff, if every guy who got dumped by his girlfriend killed her, there wouldn't be any girls left. Let's look at this another way. Kate left Marten's at ten and was alive at least until midnight. Where did she go?"

"So far we have no witnesses who can place her. She might have taken a walk around town or along the river before starting back toward campus."

"What about Buddy's bar?"

"Unlikely."

"Is anything else open in Blanton at that time of night?"

Adams seemed to scan a mental picture before saying, "Just the convenience store at the gas station, and we'd know if she went there from the security camera."

"So she must have gone to Buddy's or gone home with somebody."

"Nobody from the college goes to Buddy's."

"Why not?"

"Town and gown. They aren't welcome. It would be

dangerous."

"You mean someone could get killed?"

Adams' jaw muscles flexed so hard I expected to hear something snap. "You're good with words, Dr. Noonan, and you're probably a lot smarter than I am, but you're not from around here, and you don't know how we do things." He stood up, and I almost got dizzy maintaining eye contact. "Thank you for the information."

"Sheriff Adams, please!" He stopped in the doorway. "I'm sorry. I didn't mean to offend you. I just want the real killer to be caught, and I know you want that too. I won't get in your way."

He nodded, said, "Ma'am," and left my office.

I closed my door, locked it, and turned my chair to look out over the hillside. He was right. I didn't know how things were done around here. How could I? I came from a city where most people were not "from around here." In San Francisco, when you met someone, the first thing you asked was, "Where are you from?" because most people, it seemed, had moved to town from somewhere else. Now I was living on the side of a mountain where some English families arrived 200 years ago, some German families arrived 150 years ago, and almost everyone was descended from them. I could not even begin to imagine what it was like to grow up in such a community.

So, I didn't know how things were done around here, but I knew how to ask questions, gather facts, and draw conclusions, because that's what my education was all about. That didn't mean I was smarter than Sheriff Adams, but it did mean I could see things folks from around here might miss. I saw that Kate must have gone to Buddy's Bar, and I hoped I had given the sheriff a reason to look into that possibility.

I also saw that the muralist had hidden clues to the history of the commune among the details of his painting and that Jacob wanted to steal Kate's idea about "what one of the coffins in the mural might mean." I wasn't going to let him get away with that. I had the afternoon free, and the library was open.

I had read Jacob's book about the Eden Commune twice and it had told me nothing that would shed light on the meaning of the spotted child. It was time to look elsewhere. If other communes used such an image, I might find other sources of information about what it meant. A skeleton, for instance, is an image of horror in the gothic tradition, but a symbol of reverence for ancestors in Mexican tradition. Perhaps I could find out whether a spotted child meant something in the tradition of communes in southern Ohio during the mid-nineteenth century.

I made a list of other communes to investigate. Jacob had said Fuchs was probably influenced by John H. Noyes and the Oneida Commune as well as by the Shakers. Lionel had spoken similarly about George Rapp as a contemporary of Fuchs and about phalanxes based on the philosophy of Charles Fourier.

So, on that lovely Sunday afternoon in the college's library, I did what I usually do when faced with a subject that is new to me. I typed names and subject words into the catalogue to see what would come up.

Chapter 24

There was a lot of information on Oneida and on the Shakers in the library's catalogue, but not much on the rest. In our first conversation on the subject, Jacob had said Oneida was "different in many ways." That sounded intriguing, so I jotted down the titles of some books on it along with the call numbers and hit the stacks.

There are few things more satisfying than wandering through a library's collection, picking up books you are looking for and finding others along the way, stacking them on a table by a large window, flipping through them for a few hours, and comparing what they have to say on a subject. We take this for granted, but this is a luxury enjoyed by relatively few people in human history. Perhaps only since the institution of public libraries have most people had ready access to collected records of the thoughts and experiences of the human race.

Jacob was right. The Oneida Commune was unusual in many ways. For one thing, it went beyond providing a secure, comfortable life for its members by pursuing profit-making enterprises. For another, it encouraged its members to educate themselves and develop artistic talents. Most notably, its founder, John H. Noyes, wrote about Oneida's successes and failures, researched the progress of neighboring communes, and published newsletters that circulated to communes throughout the East and Midwest.

I discovered one other unusual quality of life at Oneida that seemed to overshadow the others. Although it was not unusual for communes at this time to practice complex marriage, in which men and women had sexual relations with more than one partner, Oneida took this practice a step further. Noyes developed a theory of "stirpiculture," a word he made up to describe breeding human beings in order to improve the species, just as farmers had bred livestock for thousands of years.

In the twentieth century, this came to be called eugenics and was among the horrors practiced by the Nazi regime. It was not entirely benign as practiced in the Oneida community: Noyes and a handful of those closest to him were considered the most promising breeders and given access to the greatest number of sexual partners.

When my eyes became tired and I had to stop reading, I took a walk around the campus to ponder what I had read, and that's when the real thinking began. At first glance, the history of Oneida did not appear to contain anything relevant to my problem. The Eden Commune was never entrepreneurial as Oneida was, and the only evidence of intellectual or artistic life at Eden was the mural in the chapel. Fuchs was not a promoter like Noyes. I had seen no evidence of complex marriage at Eden.

This phase of research is like working a jigsaw puzzle. You just keep trying different pieces in different combinations until something fits. When I asked myself if any of the things I knew about the Eden Commune were consistent with the deliberate breeding of human beings, something clicked.

What if the recurring, recognizable figures in the mural—Fuchs, Mr. Long Hair, and Smiling Woman—represented lines of breeding? The long-nosed man in the preaching scene had to be Fuchs, but the long-nosed men in the orchard and harvest scenes might represent offspring. Mr. Long Hair in the building scene would have been one of the original members of the commune, but the long-haired man in the harvest scene might be his son. Smiling Woman in the choir scene would also be first generation, but the smiling woman in the cooking scene could be her daughter, and the smiling man in the orchard scene might be her son. The muralist may have been keeping track of those who were deliberately bred, including the two children in the coffins, one long-nosed and one long-haired.

As my mind traced this pattern, my step quickened, and soon I was all but running back to my Hutch to break out my notebook, get all this on paper, and start a new list of research questions. When I got inside, I stopped long enough to put the kettle on for tea. As I wrote, it occurred to me that this new theory suggested a different motivation for Jacob to get Kate's notebook without telling me. Perhaps he knew or suspected eugenics had been practiced at Eden and wanted to keep a lid on it.

The thrill that came from my idea was tempered by remembering that I had no way to prove this. I would have to find other evidence that confirmed my interpretation of the recurring figures in the mural. I still had a lot of information to sift pertaining to Oneida, the Shakers, and others, and that could keep me busy through the end of the semester. There had to be a way to speed up the process.

Perhaps I could pick Lionel's brain about the communes he had mentioned, now that I knew what I was looking for. It couldn't hurt to ask, and I could also check on the status of our plans for a trip to Cincinnati on the coming weekend. If Lionel had returned from his weekend in New York with his parents, I would invite him over for a snack.

Lionel didn't return my call that Sunday evening, but to my delight on Monday morning I found an email from him inviting me to his apartment that afternoon at five o'clock. He suggested I "come by for a snack" and said he would be happy to share what he knew about communes. I wrote back and said I'd see him at five.

Stepping into his duplex on Ohio Avenue reminded me that, though it was just around the corner from the Rabbit

Hutches it was a world away in terms of comfort. These were real houses, built of brick, with hardwood floors and full-size appliances in the kitchen.

He welcomed me with that winning smile, and a social hug. After taking my coat, he said, "Make yourself comfortable," excused himself, and disappeared into the kitchen.

I paused by the shelving along one side of the living room to look at his array of photos in silver frames. The hairstyles and clothes told me that some of these must be portraits of great-grandparents. They looked like sophisticates of the Harlem Renaissance. A man in another photo would have been a grandfather in a U.S. Army uniform of the World War II era. The rest documented the progress of Lionel's family through the decades, concluding with a recent photo of him and, I assumed, his sister, her husband, and children.

He came back from the kitchen with a platter of cheese, crackers, and fruit. "Could I interest you in a glass of wine? I have a nice sauvignon blanc chilled."

"Thank you very much," I replied.

He returned to the kitchen, and I kicked off my shoes and folded myself onto one end of the love seat. He came back from the kitchen, this time with two glasses of wine. He set one on the coffee table in front of me and took the other with him to the oak armchair facing me.

"How is your father?" I asked.

Lionel looked surprised for a moment before he said, "He's doing fine. It was all routine. He just needs to be patient now, and that will be the hardest part for him."

I smiled and took a sip of the wine, which was tasty, and reached for a cracker and some cheese.

"What was it you wanted to discuss?" he asked.

"The day we went to Yellow Springs, you said Felix Fuchs was influenced by the leaders of other communes. I've done some reading on Oneida and have come up with some things that are helping me understand the mural here on campus."

"Sounds interesting."

"But I've hit a dead end. So, I'm wondering if you can give me a lead on where to look next."

"I will if I can. What have you discovered so far?"

"Well, you're familiar with the history of Oneida, right?"

"The main points."

"Then you know they practiced free love."

"Yes, they were well known for that, although many communes did the same. Free love grew out of the feminist movement of the early 1800s. Back then 'free love' meant that a man and woman should be able to love one another free of the bonds of marriage, because marriage meant the woman became the man's property."

"Did you also know they practiced 'stirpiculture?'"

Lionel squinted and shook his head, apparently unfamiliar with the term.

"It's a word John H. Noyes made up. It's also called eugenics."

"What? Like the Nazis?"

"Yes. Selective breeding of human beings."

He took a deep breath and sipped some wine. "I have never read anything about this."

"The descendants of those who lived in the Oneida commune weren't eager to publicize it, but materials have been released in the past few years. The diary of a young woman was recently published. In it she details her experience being selected to breed with one of the leaders of the commune."

"Oh, my goodness." He marveled at the idea. "Let me guess. The men selected as most fit to breed were Noyes and the other decision makers in the commune."

"That seems to have been the way it worked out."

"So really it was just an excuse for the older men to have sex with younger women."

"I suppose, although, since they thought men and women

became leaders because they were intellectually and spiritually advanced, they had a nobler explanation for what they were doing."

Lionel laughed. "It always helps to have a good story. Did you say this is helping you understand the mural in the chapel?"

"I noticed there's a preacher with a long nose. Jacob suggested it was Felix Fuchs. Then I noticed long-nosed men elsewhere in the mural. At first I thought this represented Fuchs playing various roles in the community, but now I wonder if the other long-nosed men represent sons. Also, there are three other recognizable individuals in the mural who turn up in several scenes. When I read about selective breeding at Oneida, I started to wonder if the muralist wasn't keeping track of the offspring of such a practice."

"Evidence of eugenics in the Eden Commune—that is a significant discovery. What does Jacob say about this?"

"I haven't told him. It's a long story, so I won't go into it, but I think he's been monitoring my work on this and wants to suppress it."

Lionel thought about that while he sipped his wine and savored it. "I could believe that. Jacob is protective of the reputation of Fuchs and the commune. That's understandable. It's his family's history too."

"I will get around to asking him about it, but I want to have my evidence all lined up first, so he can't deny it."

"I see. How can I help?"

"The day we went to Yellow Springs, you mentioned the leaders of some other communes that you thought might have influenced Fuchs. Can you tell me a little about them?"

He looked sheepish. "You'll have to remind me."

"You said one of them brought followers from Germany."

"Oh, yes. George Rapp. I'm not sure how his dates line up with Fuchs. He had some extraordinary ideas, but I'm not sure he was very influential in the long run."

"And there was a French philosopher."

"Charles Fourier. His ideas influenced many people who came to North America, and they established sustainable communities called phalanxes. He had some brilliant ideas and some crazy ones, but I don't recall anything about eugenics."

"I'm also working on another problem," I said. "The muralist included clusters of coffins as if keeping track of who died."

Lionel thought for a moment. "I've never noticed that. Of course, it's been over a year since I was in the chapel."

"They're up near the ceiling, hidden among the leaves of the tree, not easy to see. You need binoculars. Anyway, in each coffin there is a figure of a man, woman or child, with very little to distinguish them. But in one coffin is a child who seems to have spots all over him."

"Maybe that indicates the death was caused by measles or some other childhood disease."

"Possibly, but none of the other figures shows a cause of death. I'm wondering if it symbolizes something."

He pursed his lips and thought about it. "Nothing comes to mind, but if I think of anything I'll send it to you. Meanwhile I could give you a couple of references on Fourier. The library has one book in particular that's good for getting an overview of his thought."

"That would be terrific. Right now, I just need to cut down on the amount of material I have to sift through."

As I spoke, Lionel stifled a yawn. "Excuse me," he said as he stood up. "I got back from the airport late last evening and didn't sleep well. I'll just go and write down those titles."

He left the room, and I took the hint. I got up, slipped my shoes on, and went to the stand by the door where he had hung my coat. While slipping it on, I noticed some papers on the cabinet along with a ring of keys and a handful of coins. One of the papers was an itinerary for flights to and from Chicago. The return flight was dated yesterday. He had not gone to New York over the weekend. He had gone to Chicago. He had lied to me. I was stunned.

Chapter 25

"Here you are," said Lionel as he walked back into the room. He handed me an index card with three titles written on it along with the authors' names. "That first one would be the best place to start for Fourier."

I did my best to adopt a pleasant expression. "Thanks so much. I'll keep you posted on my progress."

"Please do." He smiled, but somehow it didn't warm me as it usually did.

We shared another social hug, and I left his apartment.

As I walked down Ohio Avenue, I buttoned my coat all the way up and wished I'd brought along a hat and a scarf. The autumn evenings were getting chillier.

Lionel lied to me. He told me he was going to New York when he was really going to Chicago. I fell for the oldest excuse in the academic book, the sick relative, perhaps because I never expected it from a colleague.

What was in Chicago that he didn't want me to know about? Perhaps an old girlfriend. Perhaps a new girlfriend. Perhaps a wife. Sometimes academic couples live apart when one has to move for a job, and the other has a job she can't leave.

Of course, he wasn't obliged to tell me he was in a relationship with someone else, since we weren't really starting anything serious, but he shouldn't have lied to me.

I decided to give him a day or two to tell me about his trip. If he didn't, I would put him to the test by asking if he was still interested in a trip to Cincinnati. If he still didn't come clean, I would ask him how his weekend in Chicago went.

I thought about skipping the Faculty Senate meeting at midday on Tuesday. The email from its chairman explained that the purpose of the meeting was to discuss issues arising from President Taylor's speech at the convocation two weeks ago. To me that sounded like my colleagues were getting together to blow off steam even though it wouldn't make any difference. I thought I might better use the time to get to the library and follow up on the leads Lionel had given me.

But I had to admit, I was curious about what my colleagues had to say in response to the president's call for courses and majors that prepare people for careers. Surely I was not the only one to believe that liberal arts are a preparation for any career. Lionel had been eloquent on that subject the day we went to Yellow Springs. Similar thoughts from other colleagues would go a long way to restoring my spirits.

I texted Abbie, "Senate?"

She replied, "Meet outside."

I walked over to the Old Classroom Building, but kept my distance from the entrance to the auditorium. I didn't feel like having brief conversations with people I had never met.

When I saw Abbie coming down the sidewalk from the library, I walked over and joined her. "What should I expect here?"

"Not much."

"Any advice on how to get through this?"

"Bring a book."

"You don't have one."

"It's on my phone."

As we walked toward the entrance, Abbie nodded and said good morning to a few colleagues. Behind us a couple of older gentlemen seemed to be looking forward to the meeting.

"Do you plan to introduce a resolution?" one of them asked.

"I'm undecided. You?" said the other.

"Not sure how I feel about this career-preparation business, although I suppose we have to do something. We can't just keep turning out art-history majors."

Abbie turned to confront the man, and the look on her face was scary, even to me. The elderly professor stopped dead in his tracks and his eyes searched her face and mine, apparently trying to understand how he had provoked her reaction. Sensing she was about to demand an apology, I grabbed her arm and pulled her forward with me. "Let's not do this right now," I said. She relented and followed me in.

"Art-history major" has long since become shorthand for useless knowledge, frivolous indulgence, waste of time and money, and no future. After hearing it enough times, I decided to stop fighting it and instead to apply myself to doing art history as well as I could.

The aisle seats were mostly taken, so we sat in the middle of a row, toward the back.

The chairman called the meeting to order while people were still streaming down the aisles. "President Taylor spoke to this faculty two weeks ago and gave us his reasons for changing the name of this institution when it becomes a university. No doubt some of us would like to retain the name Fuchs, while others agree with the president's reasons for eliminating it. Professor Jacob Schumacher has prepared an analysis of this issue."

The chairman sat with the other members of the Executive Committee on the stage behind the lectern. For a moment, it seemed nothing was happening, then Jacob came down the aisle from the back of the auditorium. Everyone was silent as he climbed the stairs at the side of the stage and walked to the lectern. Though dressed in his habitual costume of blue blazer, shirt and tie, and slacks, he looked impressive on this occasion. After laying out a few sheets of paper, he surveyed the assembled faculty and began to speak.

"In 1851, Felix Fuchs and his followers purchased land in these foothills and established the Eden Commune. They had left Germany where the land they worked was owned by aristocrats, and their faith was dictated to them by unscrupulous clergy. What little they had, they risked in order to live a more dignified life: a life in which their labor benefited the community, not the privileged few; in which women were treated equally with men; in which worship was a simple act of pausing in one's labor to thank God for the earth's bounty.

"Forty years later the descendants of those founding families dissolved the commune to live as individuals in the larger society of southern Ohio, but they did not leave behind the values of the commune. True to their heritage, they established the Eden Independent School, so that children from surrounding counties could receive an education. They donated much of the land from the commune to be the grounds of the school, land which they otherwise could have sold for their own profit."

I felt inspired as I listened to Jacob narrate the history of the place. Lionel was right: he had a wonderful feel for this material. Yet this was the man who went behind my back to steal my student's idea and put a stop to my research. Perhaps the college's benevolent patriarch was in fact a ruthless dictator. I couldn't allow myself to be lulled by the image he projected. I had to stay focused on replicating Kate's discovery and stopping him from calling it his own.

"In 1920, the next generation of descendants built upon this land a liberal arts college so that the young men and women of this region could continue their education without traveling far from their homes and families. And they called it Fuchs College in memory of the founder.

"Today we walk upon the same land where the members of the Eden Commune toiled, land that was dedicated, and has twice been rededicated, to helping people lead a more dignified life. We call it our campus.

"Is it important that we remember those who risked and sacrificed to make this land a place where people are raised up and set upon a higher path? Does it matter? I think it does. Otherwise how are we to emulate them and deserve their legacy?"

Jacob ducked away from the lectern and covered his mouth with one hand while the other hand reached into his pants pocket for a handkerchief. He stood with his back to us while the coughing subsided and he wiped his mouth. Everyone was silent until he returned to the lectern.

"What do we have to remind us of them? The only building left from the days of the commune is the chapel, and our new colleague in art history, Dr. Nicole Noonan, tells me its mural has much to teach us about the people who made this land their home. Beyond that, there is nothing visible to distinguish our campus from the many other liberal arts colleges in Ohio."

I have to admit, I sat up a bit straighter upon hearing my name and my work announced to one and all. "Take that, art-history bashers," I thought.

"But there is the name. 'Fuchs' is a common word in German, equivalent to the English word 'fox.' Likewise, it is commonly used as a family name. Our president is correct when he says that it can be mistaken by people whose native tongue is English, and he is right to urge caution. But I ask you, can we not teach our fellow Americans one word from another language? Can we not teach them one name from another country? Can we not make the name of this college— soon, this university—the beginning of their education?

"Or, in order to prevent an error of pronunciation, will we commit the greater error of forgetting those who walked this land before us?

"That is the question we must decide."

Jacob was impressive, and his speech earned him a warm applause.

The chairman waited while Jacob left the stage and walked back up the aisle before returning to the lectern. "Thank you, Professor Schumacher, for your thoughts on retaining the name of the college. Does anyone wish to speak in favor of eliminating the current name?"

We all waited for several seconds. No one spoke up or raised a hand.

"If no one wishes to speak, do I hear a motion to bring the matter to a vote?"

"So moved."

"Second."

"It has been moved and seconded to bring the matter to a vote. On the question of elimination versus retention . . ."

That's when I lost it. I did my best to stifle my laugh, and I think I made it sound more like a hiccup. With my hand over my mouth, I added a few coughs to disguise what was really going on, got up, and started sidestepping toward the aisle.

Abbie followed me, and, once we were outside and away from the entrance, I let out the guffaw that I'd been holding in. Abbie looked at me like I was nuts.

I waited a moment, hoping she would catch on. When she didn't, I asked, "Elimination versus retention?"

She thought about it, and chuckled. "Oh. Right. I've always said the old guard around here acts like they're constipated."

"Got time for coffee?"

"Sure."

Chapter 26

Abbie and I walked to the Student Services Center, got cups of coffee, and settled at a table overlooking the quad.

"Do you think they're going to discuss the president's plan to emphasize careers?" I asked.

"I doubt it. That's a done deal."

"I think you're right," I said. "Two weeks ago Frank asked everyone in my department to send him a memo about how we prepare people for careers. I just don't have the heart to do it. I could make a good pitch for how any career is enhanced by a knowledge of art history, but my colleagues made it clear that was not welcome. I'm supposed to tell them how studying art history gets you a job as an art historian."

"That's crazy. You can't be successful at anything by studying just that one thing. What are you going to do?"

"I may as well just write the memo. I won't be around long enough to see if it makes any difference."

"So you're searching the job market?"

"I'm about to start. I know the pickings are slim, but if I can get a couple of publications out, I'm hoping something will come along in a year or two. With any luck, I'll be gone before any of this career-orientation kicks in."

Abbie stopped and turned to me. "As you know, I keep my eye out for something better too. Whoever goes first, I'll miss you."

"I'll miss you too. We'll visit."

We hugged, and she went out the door to the patio and

walked across the lawn instead of using the sidewalks that bordered it. That must have ruffled a few feathers on the old birds who were just then spilling out of the Old Classroom Building on the west side of the quad. At least, I hoped it did.

I left the same way and took the sidewalk over to the library.

In one way, Jacob had done me a favor by mentioning me and my work in his speech. But in another way, he had given himself an advantage in the unfolding conflict between us. He now appeared to be my champion. If I ever complained about him plagiarizing a student's work and trying to obstruct my own, I would appear to be ungrateful. My strategy looked better and better: beat him to the punch.

According to the record in the library catalogue, one of the books Lionel suggested gave an introduction to Fourier's thought in only 300 pages. I found it on the shelf, and got a chair near a window. From one of the chapters I learned that in Fourier's ideal society the wealthy would live on the top floors of the four-story phalanxes while the poor lived on the ground floors. Everyone would be paid according to the value of their work, and each phalanx would be self-sustaining. When the whole world was organized this way, there would be a World Congress of Phalanxes.

In many ways, his vision of society was benign. A minimum income would be provided for everyone to live decently. Women would be in all ways equal to men; there would be no marriage contracts to bind them. Homosexual relationships would be treated no differently than heterosexual ones. Children would not be limited to playing and learning, but would be encouraged to do useful things.

However, one aspect of Fourier's vision was sinister. Since each phalanx would be self-sustaining, there would be no need for trade. Therefore, he argued, since Jews were traders, they would have no place in the new economy except as manual laborers on farms. It was shocking to see European

145

anti-Jewish bias included in an otherwise enlightened philosophy.

I read the beginnings of several other chapters and could see that they provided more detail on these topics, but I had to stop and ask myself whether any of this looked like it would help me understand the significance of the spotted child. I looked in the index for "children" and found "childhood." The main entries talked about education and appropriate work for children, but I couldn't see a connection to the image in the mural. For the moment, I couldn't see any reason to go further into the particulars of Fourier's philosophy.

The chapel was only a little out of my way as I headed home from the library, so I stopped in to sit and look at the mural for a few minutes. Low-angled sun coming in the west-facing windows made bright rectangles on the floor, which reflected a dim glow onto the mural. Details were visible on the bottom row of scenes; fewer were visible as I looked higher on the wall. The coffins were no more than shadows at the top.

As I left the chapel and waited to cross College Avenue, a car came from my right. When it rounded the curve near where I stood, the sun flashed off its windshield and momentarily blinded me. That gave me an idea.

Once across College Avenue, I picked up my pace as I walked along Ohio Avenue and was almost running as I turned onto Montgomery. I went into my Rabbit Hutch and, without stopping to take off my coat, emptied my backpack and refilled it with a notebook, sketchbook, pencil box, digital camera, and binoculars. I strapped it on, went into the bedroom, and took the long mirror from the wall.

Lucky for me, it was a simple, metallic sheet with a plastic edge, not a silvered glass mirror. Still, although it wasn't heavy, the autumn breeze caught it as I walked back on Ohio Avenue and made it awkward to carry. That and the weight in my backpack made my trip back to the chapel slower than my trip home. I was perspiring as I let myself back in.

The sunny rectangles on the floor had moved and stretched thinner, but still had power. After taking off my backpack and coat, I set the long edge of the mirror on the floor in one of the rectangles and tried reflecting the sun's light onto the mural. The effect was startling. Colors and contours leapt out at me as never before.

I experimented with different angles for the mirror and managed to reflect some light up near the roofline where the coffins were. I used a chair to hold the mirror in place and stood on another chair to give myself the best angle on the coffin with the spotted child. I lifted my binoculars to my eyes and focused.

At first I couldn't believe what I saw. The spots on the child were not just shapeless dabs of maroon paint. Each one consisted of a short, thin line with two or three thicker lines perpendicular to it. The effect was unmistakable. Each represented a slit with blood running from it. The spotted child was really a child with multiple stab wounds.

I got down off the chair and turned away for a minute. I didn't want to look at such a horrific image, but I had to do my job. After refocusing the mirror to correct for the sun's movement, I got back on the chair and looked again.

I counted nine stab wounds: one on each arm, two on each leg, and three on the abdomen. Given the muralist's simple style, I couldn't guess the child's age. He was probably old enough to walk, but not much more. The image was made more sickening by the appearance of the eyes with the lids half closed.

I stepped down again, sat, and stared at the floor in front of me to give my mind a moment to catch up with what I had seen. Was this image the record of a crime committed in the Eden Commune? A frenzied attack on a child? A murder? What else could it be?

Answering these questions would have to wait. I had one more task to complete before the late-afternoon light expired. After once more repositioning the mirror, I traded my binoculars for my digital camera and got back on the chair. I took several exposures of the overall image and used the zoom lens to get detailed photos of the face, body and legs.

The sun had just dipped behind the treetops when I left the chapel and crossed College Avenue. Parked in the drive in front of Jacob's house was a white pickup truck. I had probably seen a dozen or more like it on the roads during the two months I'd lived in southeastern Ohio and had never thought about them. But seeing this one on campus reminded me of the day I went knocking on doors near the corner of Ohio and Montgomery Avenues and heard from a neighbor that such a truck had come by in the middle of the night when the hood of my car was spray-painted.

As I approached, a man came from behind the house and put some lumber into the back of the truck. Though his cap, t-shirt, jeans, and work boots were typical for working men in the area, there was no mistaking his big arms, thick body, and aggressive posture. I remembered seeing him the day Abbie and I sat outside Emma's Deli in Blanton. It was Huey Littleton.

Chapter 24

Huey Littleton looked up, saw me, and stared as I walked by. I kept my eyes forward and did my best to ignore him.

When I was almost past Jacob's house, I glanced back, and he was gone. My insides boiled. How dare he stare me down? I was a professor on this campus. He was on my turf now.

I leaned the mirror against a tree, walked back to his truck, and waited for him to return. Within a minute, he came walking from behind the house, carrying a bucket of tools and a carpenter's level. When he looked up and saw me, he hesitated for a moment. Score one for me.

"What are you doing here?" I asked as he put the tools into the back of the truck. The moment I said it, I knew it was not my strongest opening. Obviously, he was doing some work on Jacob's house.

"Don't believe that's any of your business," he said as he closed the tailgate of the truck.

"Did you spray-paint my car?"

He said nothing as he walked to the door on the drivers' side, but his smirk was just about the ugliest expression I had ever seen on a human face.

I stepped between him and the door of the truck. "'JAP OUT?' If you don't want me here, why do you have to sneak around in the middle of the night with a can of spray paint? Why don't you have the courage to tell me to my face?"

The way his eyelids lowered, I could see he was just

about out of patience. He reached over my shoulder, grabbed the handle, and swung the door open. He would have knocked me down with it if I hadn't stepped aside.

"Were you at Buddy's Bar three weeks ago on Friday night?" I yelled as he slammed the door.

He let out a snort and sneered. "Why don't you go read a book, little girl?"

"I want to know if you saw one of my students there. Kate Conrad? Blond? About so tall?" I held up my hand about six inches over my head to indicate her height.

He squinted at me. "Come to think of it, I wasn't there that night. I was out night shooting hogs."

He revved the engine, and drove away fast enough to kick up some gravel. I managed to sidestep it.

Night shooting hogs? I don't think I had ever heard those three words in the same sentence, and I wasn't sure I wanted to know what they meant. I walked back to the tree, picked up my mirror and hurried home.

By the time I arrived at my Hutch, the afternoon light had faded to gray. I was shivering, not because of the cool air, but because my effort to confront him had failed so miserably. He didn't care if he was on my turf, or if I was a professor on this campus. I supposed that in his mind his family's history in Edwards County outweighed all that. I think my being a woman—and a small one at that—also had something to do with it. I swore I would make him pay for that "little girl" remark.

Furious as I was at his bullying, I was even more afraid his truck would come roaring down the road I lived on. After letting myself in, I locked the door, pulled all the shades, and turned on all the lights before calling Sheriff Adams. The call went to voicemail, and I said I had some information, and I was at home and concerned for my safety on campus.

When I put my phone down, I didn't feel any better. Going through my two-room house to make sure no one was hiding there took about ninety seconds. Once I knew I was alone, I turned off all the lights and peeked out from behind the shade on my front window to see if there was anyone or anything coming along the road. From my kitchen window, I scanned the tree line, which was probably thirty yards from my back door. Would I be able to see someone sneaking up on me? Only if he was carrying a big flashlight.

I jumped when my phone rang. For once, it was comforting to hear Adams' baritone drawl.

"Dr. Noonan, I got your message. Have you called campus security?"

"No."

"Hang up and call them immediately. Once you have talked to them, call me back."

I called campus security, gave them my name and address, and felt better when they said the cruiser would be there within a minute or two. I turned on some lights so the officer wouldn't find me sitting in the dark.

Was it more embarrassing to admit to myself that I was trembling in my boots or that I hadn't thought of the obvious thing to do when faced with danger on campus? Before I could sort that out, the cruiser was at my door.

This officer was not the one who had picked me up near the athletic fields a week ago Sunday. He was tall, thin, and prematurely bald. I let him in, and he stopped to take in my arrangement of beach chairs on green artificial turf.

"Why don't we sit here," I suggested, as I walked to the cafe table by the back window.

The officer joined me and took the other chair. His own weight, plus the amount of equipment strapped to him, made me wonder for a moment whether the folding chair would hold him. "I understand we have a situation here?" he asked.

"We might. A few minutes ago—maybe half an hour now—I was walking along College Avenue and I saw a pickup truck at Dr. Schumacher's house. I stopped to talk to a man named Huey Littleton, and . . . uh . . . I asked him a couple of questions. He seemed to get angry with me." Listening to myself, I was amazed at how pointless this sounded. The officer was probably already speculating about my menstrual cycle.

"Did he threaten you in any way?"

"No. He didn't actually say he was going to do anything. He just seemed really angry, and he took off in his pickup truck going really fast."

"I see," he said, making some notes. "Do you have any reason to think he will come to your home looking for you?"

My heart sped up a little, hearing those words, but I kept my voice even. "No. I don't think he will. I just got upset, and thought I should call."

"You did the right thing. I'm going to let dispatch know about this. I'm off duty at nine, but the night officer will be on the lookout for Huey's truck. If he shows up anywhere on campus this evening, we'll find out what he's up to. Also, we'll have the patrol car make an extra pass on Montgomery Avenue every hour tonight. If you notice anything that doesn't seem right, call security right away."

"I will. Thank you for getting here so quickly."

"No problem."

When he got to the door he stopped and looked at my sitting area again. "That's nice. I never would have thought of that."

I smiled. "It was cheap."

He nodded. "Looks comfortable though. Good night, Dr. Noonan."

I locked the door, put water on for tea, and called the sheriff.

After I identified myself, he asked, "Have you spoken with campus security?"

"Yes. The officer just left. It was just a precaution. Everything is under control."

"I wish everyone would take precautions instead of waiting until there's an emergency to call us. You said you had some information. Can it wait until tomorrow morning?"

"Yes. Nothing urgent. Would you like to come by my office at nine o'clock?"

"I'll see you then."

I poured hot water into the teapot, left it to steep, changed into sweatpants, and did some stretches to quiet my mind. It had been an unsettling day, but somewhere in all the chaos were some answers. I wanted to let it all go and get a good night's sleep, but that stabbed child would not be ignored.

After pouring myself some tea, I plugged my camera into my laptop, loaded the photos onto my hard drive, and saved them all to my online account. Flipping through them reminded me just how alarming the image was.

In my email account, I re-read Kate's message, sent the day before she died. She had said she used "some art-history books," the bibliography in our textbook, and some "things online" to understand "what one of the coffins in the mural might mean." Not much help there, but if she found sources that helped her understand what the image meant, it probably was not unique to the Eden Commune. Other examples were out there somewhere. I just had to find them.

In folklore, such as *Grimm's Fairy Tales*, many frightful things happen to children—baked in an oven, eaten by a wolf, and so on—but I could not think of a single one that dwelt upon the wounds and physical suffering of a child. There is plenty of blood in Christian art, especially in depictions of Jesus and the martyred saints, but I could recall only one violent incident involving children: The Massacre of the Innocents, King Herod's decree that Jewish male infants be killed in order to eliminate any potential King of the Jews who could rise to challenge his authority. There were reference books in the library in which I could survey visual treatments of this story.

Before turning in, I accomplished one more chore. I sent Lionel an email inviting him over for a glass of wine at five the next day so I could tell him how my research was going. I would also see if he would come clean about Chicago.

Chapter 28

Sheriff Adams sat in the chair by the desk in my office and leaned forward. "You did what?"

"I saw the pickup truck in front of Dr. Schumacher's house, and I went over to ask if he remembered seeing Kate at Buddy's Bar on Friday night three weeks ago."

"I have deputies who have backed down from questioning Huey Littleton," he said, a little louder than necessary.

"I wasn't questioning him." I decided to leave out the part about the spray paint on my car. "Anyway, it doesn't matter. He wasn't there that night. He says he was night shooting hogs."

Adams froze for a moment and stared at the wall before pulling out his notebook and jotting something down.

"Why would someone shoot hogs at night?" I asked.

The sheriff frowned at me. "Wild boar. These hills are full of them. Some of the boys think it's fun to hunt them at night. I don't care for it myself. The preferred weapon for hunting boar is an assault rifle. Half the time they end up shooting each other."

"Are you serious?"

"Well, not half the time, but it has happened."

"I guess you could ask whoever went hunting with him to confirm his alibi."

"No need. He's lying."

"How do you know?" I asked.

"Weather's been cool. The boar can feed during the day.

No reason for them to be active at night."

I had to admire the sheriff's grasp of the local lore. "So maybe Huey was really at Buddy's Bar the night Kate was killed, and he's trying to hide it. He might know something that would tell us who the real killer is."

"It's possible. I'll look into it. By the way I called Teresa Zannetti. She agreed to talk to me so long as it remained confidential. She confirmed what you said. Devon Manus did not abuse her when they were in high school."

"This changes everything. You can clear Devon now. He didn't do it, and it looks like Huey Littleton was involved."

"Hold on," he said. "This does not mean that Manus didn't commit the murder. It's one less reason to suspect him, but it does not clear him."

"Sheriff, you have to tell him and his parents that he's no longer under suspicion so he can return to school. He's in danger of losing a semester."

"That's not how it works," said Adams.

"But now there are other suspects. If Littleton is lying about being at Buddy's the night Kate was killed, he must think admitting he was there would make him look guilty. That means she must have been there. Littleton or someone who was at Buddy's Bar that night must have killed Kate. You said yourself it would be dangerous for someone from the college to go there."

"Please do not quote my own words to me. I said I would look into it, and I thank you for the information."

"There have to be people who saw her there. If Huey Littleton was there. . . ."

"Dr. Noonan, I want you to understand what is happening. By going after Littleton, you may have started something. His people and people from the college have been feuding off and on for a long time."

"Then why would Jacob hire Huey to work on his house?"

"The English and the Germans have lived alongside each

other and done business with each other for 150 years. But when somebody gets out of line, people choose up sides to settle it. If this gets out of hand, I cannot guarantee your safety. So, think very carefully about what you do next. I hope you will decide to stay out of it and let me do the investigating."

He stood up, nodded, and left my office.

Feuding? Adams was right. I wasn't from around here, and I didn't understand the world I had moved into. I was wasting my time trying to identify the murderer. My time would be better spent researching Kate's discovery, and announcing it to the campus.

Byron Hawley followed me to my office after art history class on Wednesday morning, saying he wanted to talk about his paper on the mural. Since it had been only a week and a half since I handed out instructions for this assignment, he deserved points for initiative.

Once seated by my desk, he pulled from his backpack a stack of pages held by a binder clip and handed them to me. "Maybe you could just take a look at these," he said.

Flipping through them, I could see he had looked up relevant topics like "mural" and "commune" on Wikipedia and other websites and printed out the articles. "It looks like you've done some research," I said.

"So, is that okay then?" he asked.

I didn't understand his question, so I ignored it. "Do you recall I suggested you come up with a topic? Did you give that some thought?"

He grinned. "Sure. The mural."

"Yes, but what about the mural?"

Still grinning, he shrugged.

I set his pages on the corner of my desk where he could reach them. "These articles should be helpful when you've decided what aspect of the mural you want to write about. Is there something about the mural that's especially interesting to you?"

"Just . . . the whole thing."

"That might be why you're having trouble getting started. Do you remember when we talked about common knowledge? If you say a mural is painted on a wall, communes were formed in the early 1800s, and the Eden Commune had a mural, that's all common knowledge, so you aren't saying much. Your topic needs to be more specific."

His eyes wandered to the scene outside my window. He looked up when I stopped speaking. "I told you I was going to need some help with this paper."

"Yes, I remember."

He slid the pages on my desk closer to me. "So, can you help me out?"

"I am trying to help you by suggesting you focus on a topic."

He scowled. "What I mean is, can you help me out the way I helped you?"

"With my car?"

His expression brightened, and he nodded.

"Are you saying you want me to write your paper for you?"

That seemed to shock him. "No. I wouldn't ask you to do that." He tapped his fingers on the pages. "You can see I've done some work here. I was hoping you could give me credit for that."

"Do you mean give you credit for writing a paper because you copied some articles?"

"Basically, yeah."

I held back from yelling at him. "That was not our understanding. There was never any agreement to trade favors."

He had that look that babies get when they're expecting a spoonful of applesauce and they get strained carrots instead. "But I helped you, so it only seems right you should do something for me."

"No, Byron, that does not seem right. Here's what I will

do. I will find out how much a shop would charge to remove spray paint, and I will write you a check for that amount. In the meantime, take these pages with you, think of a topic, and write a short paragraph defining it. When you've done that, come back and I will help you write your paper."

He snatched the pages from my desk and stalked out of my office.

I locked up my office and went out for a walk, taking the long way around to the snack bar at the Student Center to pick up a sandwich.

I had been a fool to believe Byron when he said he wanted to remove the spray paint because he didn't want me to think badly of the school. I felt sad and sickened by his attempt to manipulate me. I didn't want to become cynical, but it was becoming very hard to find anything at Fuchs College I could believe in.

Chapter 29

Perhaps because of Abbie's pep talk both my art history class that morning and my art appreciation class that afternoon felt less like burdens. I almost enjoyed them. I could feel myself giving up the idea of sharing what I loved about art history and instead meeting the students on their own level and giving them a pleasant and informative experience. Providing a service was less satisfying than teaching a discipline, but I began to think I could live with it until a better job came along.

When I got to the library shortly before three, I found Gertrud Schiller's *Iconography of Christian Art* in the reference section and looked up "Massacre of the Innocents." It showed me how that story has been represented in paintings, sculptures, mosaics, and all kinds of visual art since the middle ages.

It also showed me detailed photos of works of art from the walls of churches, the pages of illuminated manuscripts, and the panels of triptychs. None of them included a wounded child.

Instead, Christian artists had traditionally caught the horror of the incident by creating a crowd scene in which mothers fought with soldiers wielding swords. In each example, the babies were tiny details. There was no focus on the wounds as there was in the mural.

Just to be sure, I looked in the index under "child" and "children," hoping to find a subhead such as "with wounds." I also looked under "wounds" hoping for a subhead such as "child with." I found nothing.

I also consulted the *The Encyclopedia of Comparative Iconography*, which does not limit itself to Christian art. Again, I found no image similar to the one in the mural.

Since I hadn't gotten lucky with either of these general iconographies, I needed a more specific reference. I fantasized about finding a book about murals in the chapels of nineteenth-century American communes, and searched for it, but there didn't seem to be such a thing, even through interlibrary loan.

Using the library's catalogue, I did a keyword search for "iconography" and found several in the collection: *Pagan Celtic Britain: Studies in Iconography and Tradition*; *Route 66: Iconography of an American Highway*; *Dark Mirror: The Medieval Origins of Anti-Jewish Iconography*; and *Medieval Spanish Iconography* among others. None of these was especially promising for my present project, but, so the afternoon wouldn't be a complete loss, I checked out *Pagan Celtic Britain* and *Dark Mirror* so I could peruse them at my leisure and add them to my database of research tools.

It was after four, and I needed to prepare for Lionel's visit. I went home, swept the floor, wiped down the bathroom, put all my extra books back on their shelves, and made sure no stray items of clothing had wound up under the bed or in otherwise embarrassing places.

As I worked, I pondered the sorry state of my research. Kate somehow discovered a meaning for the image of the stabbed child, and she did so partly with materials in the college library. Therefore, the answer was on a page in a book within my reach, but without knowing all the links in the chain that led her to that page, it was lost to me. I needed to speed things up. Although Jacob would need months to get an article ready to send to a journal, I wanted to be sure I announced Kate's discovery to the campus before he could use it as his own.

I was trying to think of a way to break the deadlock when I heard a knock at my door.

Lionel's arrival at my place for a snack and a chat at five o'clock on Wednesday was a mirror-image replay of my arrival at his place on Monday afternoon. We had the social hug at the door, I took his coat and told him to get comfortable. As I got the cheese plate and a bottle of wine out of my tiny fridge, I said, "You were right about that book on Fourier. It was just what I needed."

"I'm glad to hear that."

"It's amazing to think of people in Europe crossing an ocean to build utopian communities based on a plan proposed by a French philosopher."

Lionel nodded. "I think the real incentive was the availability of land, which at that time was the source of all wealth. The philosophers and preachers just gave them a road map."

I set the snack and the drinks on the little table between the beach chairs and sat opposite him. "Fourier's phalanx system has a lot in common with the other communes when it comes to women's equality, social welfare, and so on."

Lionel sipped some wine. "They were carrying out the philosophy articulated in the previous century by Rousseau, Voltaire, Diderot and others—the Age of Enlightenment."

"That makes sense, but on one point Fourier doesn't seem too enlightened. He says that since self-sustaining phalanxes won't need to trade, Jews would be useful only as manual laborers on the farms."

Lionel winced. "He wasn't right about everything. Was any of this helpful with that image you found in the mural? Something about a child?"

"No, but there has been a development on that. I was able to look at the mural under stronger light, and I discovered the spots on the child are actually stab wounds."

Lionel leaned forward in his chair, as if by getting closer to me he could examine more closely what I was saying. "Stab wounds? Are you sure?"

"There are nine slits on the child's torso, arms and legs. Each has blood running from it."

"That's bizarre. How old is this child?"

"It's hard to tell. Maybe around two. Have you ever seen anything like that? Or can you think of any place in literature where the idea of a wounded child symbolizes something?"

He shook his head. "This does not ring any bells."

"I haven't been able to find a reference to such an image, but there must be a precedent, because my student sent me an email right before she died saying she had found something that suggests what it means."

"But she didn't say what?"

"No."

Lionel set his glass on the side table and leaned back in his chair. "Very mysterious. I'm afraid I can't help you with that."

"Perhaps you can help me with something else. How was your trip to Chicago?"

I had never in fact seen a deer in headlights, but Lionel must have been doing a good imitation of one as he sat staring at me. I didn't enjoy watching him suffer, so I said, "Your itinerary was on the cabinet by your door in plain sight when I was leaving your place Monday afternoon."

He closed his eyes for moment and exhaled. "I was trying to decide when to tell you about that. I was short-listed for a position at Northwestern. I went there for a job interview."

"Good for you, but why lie about it?"

He bowed his head and spoke softly. "I didn't say anything before I went for the interview because I didn't want to make an issue out of something that might not happen."

"When were you going to mention it?"

"I wanted to see how the interview went and try to figure out if I was still in the running for the job."

"Are you?"

He sighed. "I haven't heard anything."

"I still don't see why you wanted to keep it secret."

"I was afraid you might lose interest if you thought I'd be leaving next summer, and I didn't want to miss my chance with you."

That was awfully sweet. Still, he lied to me. "I can't decide which is worse, you using the sick-parent excuse or me falling for it."

"I'm sorry. I should have talked to you about it before I went for the interview. And I definitely should not have lied about it and said I was going to New York. Believe it or not, I do know that the foundation of any relationship is honesty. If you give me another chance, I promise I will never again hold anything back."

After taking a moment to think about it, I asked, "Can we talk tomorrow?"

"Of course."

"It's probably okay, but there's been so much going on I don't know what to think right now."

"And, don't forget, you are in your first semester in a new job in an unfamiliar part of the country."

"Thanks for reminding me."

"I'd better go."

I followed him to the door and pulled him in for a real hug. He didn't resist.

"I'll call you tomorrow," I said.

He replied, "I look forward to it," and left.

So, all this time he really was thinking about getting serious with me, but he didn't want to start something he couldn't finish. Along with his other fine qualities, he was considerate. Maybe I'd been overthinking this. It was possible we both would spend the next few years here, and beyond that, who knew? I needed a good night's sleep before I could think about this anymore.

Later that evening, Sheriff Adams called. "Good evening, Dr. Noonan. I have an update for you on the situation we discussed this morning. We have reason to believe that Huey

Littleton had contact with Kate Conrad at Buddy's Bar on the evening before she died."

Chapter 30

"Are you saying Huey Littleton murdered Kate Conrad?" I asked. "Are you going to arrest him?"

"We're going to bring him in for questioning," said Sheriff Adams, "but we have to find him first. I'm calling to ask for your cooperation."

I wondered for a moment if he was being sarcastic, but decided to give him the benefit of the doubt. "All right. How can I cooperate?"

"Are you at home right now?"

"Yes."

"Do you have plans to go out this evening?"

"No."

"Then I would ask you please to stay home and make sure your doors and windows are locked. I have asked the campus police to contact my department if they see Littleton. I would ask you to do the same. If you see him or his truck, or if you have any reason to think he is nearby, please call me. If you notice anything unusual in your neighborhood, call the campus police immediately. I have already asked them to increase patrols in your area of the campus. Do I make myself clear?"

"Yes. Entirely clear, Sheriff."

"Thank you."

"Sheriff? One other thing: Will you call me when you have talked to him?"

He took so long to answer that I thought we might have been disconnected. "Yes. I'll give you a call."

I hung up, checked the locks on my doors and windows, and pulled all the shades down. There wasn't much daylight left anyway. I didn't have much of an appetite, but I forced myself to stir-fry some vegetables and tofu. I knew I couldn't concentrate on anything demanding, so, after I ate, I poked around in my closet and found the thriller I had bought at the airport when I flew out here in August. I had read only half of it on the plane. I was still awake when I finished it after midnight. I fell asleep sometime after that.

I was in better shape than I had expected as I went off to teach art appreciation on Thursday morning, and I enjoyed the class. We seemed to have reached an unspoken agreement. They would volunteer comments in class so long as I kept my expectations low and told them what would be on the exam and how to get an A.

I was in a reasonably good mood when I got to my office after class and took a call from Sheriff Adams. "Good morning, Dr. Noonan. I need to meet with you."

"Of course. What time?"

"I'm on campus now, if you're available."

"Yes. I'm in my office."

"I'll be right over."

In the few minutes before he arrived, I felt more and more energetic. He wouldn't make a trip to campus if there weren't some development in the case. He probably had caught Huey Littleton and questioned him. Maybe Huey had confessed. I was standing at my window, looking out over the treetops, which now reflected the morning sun in shades of orange, yellow and red, when I heard a tap at my door.

Sheriff Adams kept his eyes down as he greeted me and took a seat. Maybe the news was not so good after all.

"Thank you for seeing me right away, Dr. Noonan. I thought you would like to know we have Huey Littleton in custody."

"Thank you, Sheriff. That's a relief. Has he confessed to

the murder?"

Adams looked surprised at that. "Why would you think that?"

"I thought you said you arrested him."

He sat back in his chair. "We arrested him because he tried to take down two of my deputies."

The sheriff's words hit me like a cold hand between my shoulder blades. I should never have approached Littleton directly. "Were they injured?"

"Just a little roughed up. They'll be fine. Anyway, we were up half the night getting a statement from him. I'm letting you know personally because when all this becomes public . . . well, it could have an impact."

I started to ask what impact, but decided he would get to it more quickly if I just waited.

"Based on Littleton's statement, and statements from others who were at Buddy's Bar that Friday evening, we have a clear sequence of events. Littleton arrived around eleven thirty and parked his truck in the lot behind the bar. As he approached the rear entrance, he heard voices and walked over to see who was there. Between two cars parked close to the wall of the building he found Kate Conrad and another young woman—her name is being withheld for the time being—and they were engaged in an unnatural act." He looked me in the eye for the first time since he walked into my office.

It took me a moment to understand what he was saying. "They were having sex?"

A look of disgust flickered across Adams' face. "The two women ran into the bar. . . ."

"What? Why would they go in there?"

"I imagine it seemed safer than having Littleton chasing them down a dark alley."

"Of course. Excuse me. Please, go ahead."

"Littleton followed them in and yelled for the other young woman to go home. When he tried to lay hands on Ms. Conrad, several men in the bar restrained him and yelled for her to get out. Ms. Conrad left by the rear entrance. Littleton left the bar a short time later." Adams ended his story with his eyes focused on the floor, away from me.

"So, it would seem you have a new suspect."

He was obviously fatigued from the long hours he had put in. "Oh, there's no shortage of suspects."

"What I mean is, Littleton was angry with her—angry enough that he had to be restrained—so he had a motive, or thought he did. He could have guessed she would use that path across the field as a shortcut back to campus, and he could have been waiting for her when she got to Route 212."

He shook his head. "If he wanted to kill her, why wouldn't he just catch up with her on the path? He'd have a more secluded place to do it."

The sheriff had a point, but following his logic I saw another possibility. "Maybe he did follow her up the path, and she ran, and he caught up with her where the path meets the road."

"Unless Ms. Conrad was an athlete, I have to think he would have caught her long before they got to the road."

I couldn't recall Kate saying anything about sports, but I hadn't known her that long. "You can clear Devon now, can't you? It has to be Littleton, doesn't it?"

"You seem to be overlooking something, Doctor. The young lady that Ms. Conrad was . . . uh . . . involved with behind the bar has a family here in town. We're still trying to determine whether her father or either of her brothers was at the bar that night. Any or all of them might have gone after your student. Around here, people don't like that sort of thing."

I had to catch my breath. "What sort of thing? What are you saying?"

"I'm saying your student wasn't entirely innocent in this series of events."

I felt my heart pumping. "She certainly was innocent."

"If somebody comes into a town like this, and has that

kind of influence on the young people, there's going to be trouble."

I had to grip the arms of my desk chair to keep myself from standing up and yelling at him. "'That kind of influence?' Are you saying she deserved to be killed?"

"No, I am not, and when I have enough evidence I will make an arrest and send the case to the prosecutor. Meanwhile, I am giving you the courtesy of letting you know what your student did before it becomes public. I promise you, once it does come out, there will be outrage."

"There is already outrage over the murder of a fine, young woman."

"All right then," said Adams, as he stood up. "Don't bother to thank me," he said, and he was gone.

My mind was racing, but no matter how many times I asked myself, "What just happened here?" the answer came back the same. Adams was blaming Kate for bringing violence upon herself. Would he have said a young man was less-than-innocent because he engaged in a "natural act" with a young woman behind a bar? Well, maybe he would. Fathers, brothers, and neighbors can be protective of young women. But in that instance, he wouldn't say "that sort of thing" and "that kind of influence," and he would not anticipate outrage from the community.

Since there were no students waiting to talk to me, and I had no afternoon class, I cancelled the rest of my office hour and headed home. All the way back, my mind was whirling. So, Kate was gay. Did she understand that or was that evening's encounter something done on impulse, to see what it felt like, perhaps after a few beers?

The idea that she may have been killed in a hate crime made all this worse. I swore to myself I would make sure the subhuman who took her life was charged with everything possible. If Adams was too squeamish to protect the rights of a gay woman, I would organize protesters and lead a parade down the main street of Blanton carrying signs that said

"Justice for Kate Conrad."

By the time I got back to my Hutch, I felt ready to explode. Though I hadn't planned to run that day, I put on my running gear and headed out to the athletic fields, determined not to come back until I was ready to drop from exhaustion.

Chapter 31

After a shower, I put on pajamas and decided to call Lionel before I settled in for the remainder of the afternoon and the evening. My mind and my heart were no more settled than when we talked the day before, but I had promised to call. He answered on the second ring.

"Nicole, how are you?"

"Exhausted, confused, and sad."

"Would you like me to come over? I could run into Blanton for some take-out food. "

"I'll have to say no thanks for this evening," I said, "although I think we should have dinner together soon. The investigation into Kate Conrad's death has taken some strange turns this week, and that's been upsetting for me."

"I'm sorry to hear that."

"Thank you. Please don't think this is because of our misunderstanding about you going away last weekend. I should not have jumped to the conclusion you had someone else in your life."

"It was my fault, really."

"Not entirely. I could have saved us both a lot of grief if I had asked you why you went to Chicago as soon as I saw that itinerary. But we'll get over that. Let's have dinner someplace Friday evening. Or maybe we could just drive up to Columbus on Saturday."

"That sounds like fun. We can finalize plans tomorrow."

"Thanks. I hope I'll be able to think clearly then."

We said goodnight and I hung up and switched off the ringer of my phone. For the rest of the evening, whatever happened could wait until tomorrow unless it involved fire engines pulling up in front of my Hutch. I put on some music, heated up some soup, and buttered a slice of bread, but my mind kept going over that conversation I'd had with Sheriff Adams.

To give myself something else to think about, I grabbed the books I had borrowed from the library and brought them to the table. *Pagan Celtic Britain: Studies in Iconography and Tradition* had caught my eye because Dad is always calling things Celtic, including music and dance. I try to tell him the Celts were a prehistoric people, and very little is known about them, certainly nothing about their music. He just rolls his eyes, and says I need to learn more about my heritage.

The other book, *Dark Mirror: The Medieval Origins of Anti-Jewish Iconography*, caught my eye because its title made me recognize that we art historians spend almost no time on works of art that are hateful. We label them as "propaganda" and try to forget about them. Growing up in San Francisco, I was taught about the Chinese Exclusion Act, a federal law which restricted immigration by Chinese people from 1880 to 1943, but I could not recall learning about art created during that time such as cartoons and posters that would have encouraged the bias written into that law.

With such thoughts whirling in my head, I scanned the table of contents, and read the introduction. The author's thesis, suggested in the title, was that the distorted and cruel depictions of Jews in the Middle Ages reflected anxieties within the Christian community over its own identity. I flipped through the pages, reading a paragraph here and there, especially at the beginnings of chapters, and stopping to look at pictures.

As I did so, by accident I found what I had been seeking the past two days. There, at the top of page 227, was a drawing of a child perhaps two or three years old, lying dead, covered with stab wounds. I couldn't sit still so I got up and paced around my two rooms while holding the book in front of me and reading about the history of this revolting image. It was an example of blood libel, a recurring theme in the history of European anti-Semitism. This lie made Christians believe that Jews would kidnap their children, and then torture and kill them. In some versions, Jews supposedly did this to re-enact the crucifixion of Christ; in others, they supposedly did it to obtain blood for rituals.

By the time I had read several pages about false accusations of ritual murder, and had looked at other examples of this image, my knees were weak. I am not sure which was more shocking: the hideous nature of the slander or my own ignorance of this history. I had read dozens of books and heard hours of lectures about European art, and I had learned enough European history to understand that art in its original context, but never before had I seen any hint of this.

As I absorbed the shock of this discovery, I began to think about what it meant. I now knew that the muralist who was part of the Eden Commune had included in his "tree of life" an anti-Jewish image that had deep roots in the European tradition from which Fuchs and his followers came.

Since I also thought that the recurring figures in the mural were evidence of eugenics, I was on the verge of proving that members of the commune were in some ways forerunners of the Nazis. This was like finding out that someone's family had been slave owners, or had participated in the genocide of Native Americans.

No one at Fuchs College would thank me for publishing this information. It was hard to imagine they would even tolerate my presence. Forget about tenure, they might find a way to fire me by the end of this academic year.

But I knew I could not bury my discovery, partly because I had enough of a conscience to know we all have to take a stand when we see something that's wrong, but also because the purpose of my profession is to create and share knowledge.

It would be fun to tell a friend that the painting she found in her grandmother's basement is a lost masterpiece by Edward Hopper, but the obligation is the same when the discovery brings no joy.

I did however rethink my strategy. The implications of this image were too profound to be mixed into a classroom lecture on folk art or announced to the campus in the student newspaper. I had no wish to shame the founders of the Eden Commune and by implication Fuchs College. And, though he had acted selfishly, Jacob deserved better than to have this thrown in his face. Rather than beating him at his own game, I decided to invite him once again to collaborate.

I sent him an email asking if I could drop by his house Friday afternoon.

When I walked into my art history class on Friday morning, the room fell silent. Usually they continued chatting with one another while I plugged my laptop into the room's projection system and opened my textbook and notebook on the lectern, but on this day it was so quiet by the time I got to the front of the room that I paused and looked around to see what the reason might be. No one looked up at me. Byron Hawley was bouncing one knee as he stared at the ceiling. Ursula Wilmot appeared to be reviewing notes from previous classes and checking things off in the margins. All the others rested their eyes on their desktops or on the floor. These lulls often happen around midterm, but it was early for that.

"Good morning!" I said, with a bit of extra energy, hoping to wake everyone up. "Today, we're going to find out what a flying buttress is and see how it revolutionized art in gothic churches."

Not even a flicker of interest. I had learned from one of my professors in grad school how to break through a wall of student apathy: use their own silence against them. "Who can tell me what a buttress is?" I left that question hanging in the air while I plugged in my laptop, put a slide of Notre Dame

Cathedral on the screen, and found the appropriate pages in my textbook and notebook.

When all was ready, the classroom was still about as lively as a tomb. I'm sure they thought that if they just kept their heads down long enough, I would start babbling about the glories of stained glass. Instead I folded my arms, stood my ground, and swept the room with my eyes.

After about thirty seconds, cracks began to appear in their defenses. Two women who always arrived together and sat together in the back, began glancing sideways at each other.

I knew that if I called on someone by name I would lose the battle of wills. So, I waited.

Ursula Wilmot remained fascinated by her own class notes. Byron Hawley seemed absorbed in whatever he saw on the ceiling, no doubt projections of whatever painting he was working on. Others fidgeted.

Still I waited.

One of the two in the back slipped her phone out of her purse and held it beneath the writing arm of her chair, apparently thinking that made it invisible to me. After half a minute of furious thumbing, she looked up and said, "a reinforcement of a wall or other part of a building?"

"Thank you. That's right. So why would some buttresses be described as 'flying?'" When no one replied after a moment, I added, "you can see why if you look at what is on the sides of Notre Dame Cathedral in this picture."

Most of them glanced up at the screen and then looked down at their notebooks. Once again I folded my arms, ready to wait them out. This time it took only about ten seconds to get an answer.

Most professors resent having to practice dentistry. Often they can be heard saying, as they leave the classroom, "that was like pulling teeth." I'll admit I grew tired and ended class five minutes early, but not before telling Byron Hawley I wanted to speak to him.

As the others left, he shuffled to the front of the room and waited, stone-faced, to hear what I had to tell him.

I pulled from my purse a check payable to him for the amount a shop in Chillicothe quoted me for removing spray-painted graffiti from a car. He stared at the check for a moment, and, without looking up at me, grabbed it from my hand and walked out.

Ursula Wilmot came forward, handed me a copy of the student newspaper, and said, "You should read this." I took it from her, and she left the room. I saw nothing noteworthy on the front page until I got to the lower left corner and found the headline that read, "Slain Student Had Lesbian Affair."

Chapter 32

My stomach felt like I was riding down in a very fast elevator. I hid the paper in my notebook, gathered all my things, and hurried to my office. Even there, I was afraid someone would drop by and see the look on my face while I was reading the article, so I called the department's secretary and told her I wasn't feeling well and needed to cancel my office hour and one o'clock class. She assured me she would post the appropriate notices, and I hurried out of the building.

After I crossed College Avenue into the residential section of campus where fewer people were coming and going, I stopped and texted Abbie: "My Hutch NOW."

Once inside my front door, I stood by the window and read the article:

> On the night, she was killed, Fuchs College senior Kate Conrad allegedly met a woman from Blanton for a sexual encounter behind Buddy's Bar, according to the Edwards County Sheriff's department. The name of the woman is currently being withheld.
>
> The Sheriff's department spokesman refused to speculate on whether this encounter, which was discovered by patrons of the bar, led to Conrad's death later that night. The Sheriff's department considers her death suspicious and is investigating it as a possible murder.

Conrad was known to be a favorite of art history professor Nicole Noonan, who joined the faculty this fall. Dr. Noonan has degrees from San Francisco State University and the University of California, Santa Barbara. She is a native of San Francisco, CA.

I was trying to decide whether I needed to breathe into a paper bag to stop myself from hyperventilating when I heard a rap at my door. I opened it, and Abbie stepped in.

I held up the newspaper. "Have you seen this?"

"Is that today's?"

I handed her the paper, pointed to the headline, and turned away. Leaning on the kitchen sink and looking out the window, I got my breathing under control. When I turned back, it seemed her face, paler than usual, had turned to stone.

"Did you know?" she asked.

I shook my head.

She closed her eyes and stood there holding the paper. "Where was she from?"

"Lancaster."

"Pennsylvania?"

"Ohio."

She nodded. "At least that's a decent-sized town, and it's close to Columbus."

"What do you mean?"

"More chance there was a bookstore or a church with an outreach ministry, maybe a community hotline for teenagers to call. I guess it doesn't matter now. I was just hoping she had some way of understanding herself and of talking to people who understood her. Was she out to her parents?"

"I don't know."

Abbie held up the paper. "This would be a terrible way to find out."

I poured myself a glass of milk. "Do you want anything?"

She shook her head.

We sat at the cafe table, and I took a deep breath before speaking. "This is going to sound incredibly petty, but how dare they say she was 'a favorite' of mine? I don't have favorites, and that belittles the work Kate was doing on her own."

"That doesn't sound petty. I'd say it sounds about right."

"By the way, I had a disturbing conversation about this with Sheriff Adams this morning. He came by to tell me Huey Littleton caught Kate and this local girl in the act, and that he's investigating whether Huey or someone from the girl's family may have come after Kate. The disturbing part was when he said Kate was 'not entirely innocent.' He implied that she was partly responsible for what happened to her."

Abbie made a sound in her throat as if she were gagging. Her pale cheeks were flushed with color.

"This makes me want to go crazy and throw things," I said.

"That's not a bad idea, but don't throw anything expensive," she replied.

After we sat for a minute without talking, I said, "I'm going to give the campus another way to remember her. She made a significant discovery by studying the mural in the chapel. Jacob has been trying to keep it under wraps, but I'm seeing him this afternoon, and I'm going to convince him we should find a way to publish it under her name. I want her to be remembered as a scholar."

"Good for you, Noonan," said Abbie as she stood up. "I have to go. I have a one o'clock. Are you around this weekend?"

"Yeah, although Lionel and I might drive up to Columbus on Saturday. How about you?"

"I'm not sure. I have to call Sharon tonight. We've been talking. I might go to Pittsburgh."

"That is definitely the best news I've heard all day. I hope you work things out."

"Thanks. I'll check you later."

Abbie left. I pulled the shade in my bedroom and stretched out on the futon. I needed to play some mental chess before my meeting with Jacob at three o'clock. In case my meditation turned into a nap, I set an alarm for two thirty.

I felt surprisingly good as I walked over to Jacob's house that Friday afternoon. So much had gone wrong, but I was finally in a position to do something about it. I knew what Kate had discovered, and I knew Jacob had her notebook, so I could call his bluff if he continued to pretend he knew nothing about the coffins in the mural, the stabbed child, and its significance. I hoped he would admit he had gone behind my back, agree that there was no point in suppressing Kate's discovery, and join me in preparing an article that would acknowledge her contribution to interpreting the mural.

As I turned up the walk to his front door, I could hardly believe that less than four weeks had passed since I had first visited this house. Our consultation on research in the archives seemed like something that happened in a previous lifetime, one that did not include the murder of a brilliant young woman. I wished I could turn the clock back.

Chapter 33

"Good afternoon, Nicole." Jacob welcomed me with a smile and waved me through his front door and toward the living room.

"Good afternoon, Jacob." I smiled back and walked through the archway into that lovely room with its built-in bookcases, tall windows and fireplace. I sat as I had before on the loveseat and admired once again the collection of precious Meissen porcelain in the tall glass cabinet in the corner. On the coffee table in front of me were two recent issues of a history journal and a fine old leather-bound book. It might have been a bible or a volume of Goethe. I couldn't see the spine.

Jacob paused just inside the archway and asked, "Can I get you anything? Tea? Coffee? A glass of wine?"

"No, thank you."

He sat in the armchair with its back to the door and clasped his hands over his belly. "So how is the work coming along?"

He asked this with such warm expectation that for a moment I wanted to tell him everything I knew, but I remembered Kate and proceeded to set my trap. "I'm afraid I've hit a dead end. Maybe you can help me. In the records of the Eden Commune, have you ever seen any reference to a child being murdered?"

His brow furrowed, and he said, "No. What a horrible thought! Why do you ask?"

"Hidden among the details of the mural is an image of a

child who has died from multiple stab wounds."

He gasped and raised his eyebrows. "The mural in the chapel?"

I had to purse my lips to stop myself from smiling at his attempt to seem surprised. "Yes, Jacob. I'm wondering if the muralist was documenting an actual crime committed at that time."

"I've never seen a record of any such crime, I'm happy to say. I'm surprised to hear that there is such an image in the chapel."

He had fully committed to his lie, so it was time to spring the trap. "I don't think you are surprised, Jacob. For one thing, you've read about it in Kate Conrad's notebook."

He shook his head as if clearing cobwebs. "Excuse me, what notebook are you talking about?"

"I called Kate's parents last week to ask if I could see the notebook she kept for my class. Her mother told me that you had already spoken to them, and that they had mailed it to you."

"They mailed it?" He shook his head. "I haven't received it."

Apparently, he thought that if he ignored the obvious, I wouldn't ask. "But you did call Kate's parents? Why did you want to see her notebook?"

He stared into the distance and nodded slowly. "I saw her in the library. I think that was the day after you introduced me to her in the chapel. I inquired about her work on the mural and offered to help. She said something about such an image. I must have made a note of it somewhere and then, after she was killed, I suppose I wanted to find out what she was thinking. Yes, now that I think of it, I did call her parents and ask for the notebook, but it never arrived, and I must have forgotten about it." He smiled. "There's probably a note about it on my desk, buried under a stack of other notes. You know how it is. Thank you for reminding me."

I had to give him credit for thinking fast. He took the few

facts I put before him and bent them into a story that made him look innocent. "Do you recall what she said about the image when you spoke to her in the library?" I asked.

He made a good show of thinking about it before saying, "I'm afraid not."

"What suggestions did you make?"

He held out both hands, palms up, and gave a slight shrug. "I'm afraid I don't remember things like I used to."

I did not for one moment believe his memory was failing. "Did she think the image was a record of an actual crime or did she have some other theory?"

"I wish I could remember. I suppose that's why I wanted to see her notebook. I must check with the mailroom." He glanced at his watch. "Well, it's too late now. They close early on Fridays. I'll check with them first thing on Monday. They may have forgotten to put a package slip in my box. It could be sitting there right now."

I looked him in the eye. "I think you know what she was researching from your conversation with her. I think you recognized the stabbed child for what it is, an anti-Jewish image, and did your best to throw her off the scent. I think you got that notebook from her parents to keep me from getting hold of it. Maybe you didn't want it to come out that some members of the Eden Commune carried on a tradition of bigotry that goes back to the Middle Ages. I've discovered that history on my own, and I'm going to write about it. I hope we can cooperate on this, and I hope you will work with me to make sure Kate gets credit for this discovery."

Jacob's eyelids drooped slightly, as if he were thinking more than seeing. "I don't care for the accusations you're making, but for a moment let's take a look at this idea you have. Felix Fuchs was a religious leader, but he broke with the institutional church in Germany. So, it's hard to believe he or his followers would have continued this anti-Semitic tradition that was a product of that church. Also, he was influenced by the philosophical movement called the Enlightenment. Like most of the leaders of communes in the 1800s he believed in things like the brotherhood of man and equality, so I don't think he subscribed to the belief that some people are inferior."

I sat forward on the loveseat so I could get both heels on the floor and sit tall. "Charles Fourier was also a post-Enlightenment thinker. Nonetheless, his vision of a new society said Jews were only good for manual labor on farms. European anti-Semitism did not disappear with the Enlightenment, as the history of the twentieth century tells us."

Jacob sneered and clapped his hands three times. "Well done, Dr. Noonan. You win the debate." He sat forward and braced his elbows on the arms of the chair. "You're right, of course. Your student somehow worked out the meaning of this image."

"If by 'somehow' you mean imagination, critical thinking, and research, then I agree with you."

"When I spoke to her in the library I recognized the image as typical of the blood libel against Jews, a loathsome tradition and, as you've said, a very old one. I tried to steer her in a different direction."

"Why?" I asked. "She had made a significant discovery. We could have encouraged her to write it up for publication. She might have won an award or a scholarship."

"Yes, I recognized what a rare and excellent thing she had done, but by itself such an article might have created a lot of misunderstanding. I wanted to mention it first in the biography of Fuchs that I am close to completing."

"In other words, you wanted to treat it like your own discovery."

"Not at all," he said. "I would have acknowledged her discovery, and then I would have helped her to publish her work, but first there were questions to be answered. Who was the muralist? Was it his idea to put this image in the mural? Did Fuchs know about it? I wanted to present this discovery in the context of its times. It's easy now to look back and brand someone an anti-Semite, but a hundred years before the Nazis what did this image mean?"

I did my best to keep myself from yelling at him. "I imagine it meant the same thing as it means now."

"Nicole, try to see this from my point of view. *Tree of Knowledge*, my history of the Eden Independent School, was my first book. I followed it with *Tree of Life*, telling the history of the Eden Commune, which is ultimately the source of everything we have here. My biography of Fuchs, my third book, will tell not only how he and others founded the commune but also how he became the man he was. I've researched his family in Germany and his early years there. An understanding of who he was is critical to understanding the commune, the independent school, and this college.

"This influence your student discovered is a tiny particle of that story. If it were published first, out of context, it would create prejudice about Fuchs. That would endanger the work I've dedicated my life to, just as I am about to complete it, and might jeopardize the future of the college."

"Jacob, you could have talked to me," I said. "She was doing the work for my class after all. We would have respected your point of view and the work you were doing."

"Perhaps you're right." He seemed to be tired of talking about it. "I'll go upstairs and get that notebook for you."

He stood up from his chair and said, "In fact, there was nothing respectful in her attitude. When I told her she needed guidance regarding the meaning of the image, she insisted she was right and refused to listen to reason. She said she was going to write her paper for you just as she wanted, no matter what I said. That's why I had to stop her."

He picked up the poker from among the fireplace tools, weighed it in both hands, and took a step toward me.

Chapter 34

My mind froze.

Fortunately, my body was more in the moment. As soon as Jacob stepped forward, my hand went for that leather-bound book on the coffee table, and I gave it a side-arm toss in the direction of the glass case full of porcelain in the corner. He yelled, and there were thumps and bumps, but no sound of breaking glass, so I guess I didn't hit it. I didn't see what was happening because as soon as that book left my hand I was over the back of the love seat and sprinting toward the door.

I lost a step on him because I had to pull the door open, but I made it onto the porch without being hit. It must have been close though because I heard a loud whack on the doorframe behind me.

I leaped off the porch, and ran toward College Avenue, looking both ways for cars. There was one coming from the left and one from the right. Both were moving slowly, so I kept running until I crossed the street and started up the lawn in front of the Science Building.

I risked a glance over my shoulder, saw no one, and stopped to look back. Jacob stood framed in the doorway of his Victorian house. As I watched, he backed into the house and closed the door.

Neither of the cars stopped to see why a woman had just come running out of Dr. Schumacher's house. There was no one walking along College Avenue. The campus seemed deserted, which was not unusual late on a Friday afternoon.

I needed help. I had to report what Jacob had said and done and ask for protection.

That's when I noticed I didn't have my purse. Of course: I left it on the loveseat when I made my escape.

Freaking out would not help. I had to focus on finding solutions. I could roam the halls of one of the classroom buildings hoping to find a colleague still in his or her office, but at almost four o'clock on a Friday afternoon that was unlikely. The closest place I was sure to find someone who would let me use a phone was the circulation desk of the library. With a last glance at Jacob's house, I turned and ran.

The librarian at the circulation desk, a woman in her fifties with her hair permed, wearing expensive glasses and a hiking vest, put down her pen and looked up from the list of things she was checking. "May I help you?"

I was glad to see her smile. "Yes," I said, "I've just had a disturbing experience, and I need to call the campus police, but I seem to have run off without my purse, which has my cell phone and keys in it."

"Oh dear." Her brow furrowed as she picked up the phone on the counter in front of her and punched a button. "Are you okay? Do you want to sit down?"

"I'll be fine, but I think I'll just wait here to speak to them."

She nodded, listened for a moment, and spoke into the phone. "Could you send a security officer to the circulation desk at the library? A faculty member needs assistance." She hung up and said, "They'll be right over."

I thanked her and walked to the front doors to watch for the cruiser.

What happened at Jacob's house made no sense. It sounded as if he had confessed to killing Kate, but professors don't murder students over intellectual differences. Coming at me with a poker sure looked like he wanted to kill me too, but he had no reason to do that . . . unless he didn't want anyone ever to know about the stabbed child.

The cruiser parked in the red zone at the end of the sidewalk leading to the library. No siren, but the lights were flashing. I was glad to see security taking this seriously. When the officer got out and walked toward the library, I recognized him by his premature baldness. He had come to my Rabbit Hutch the night Huey Littleton was on the loose and had shown me a lot of kindness and consideration.

As he walked through the door, he looked to the circulation desk, and the librarian nodded toward me. He changed course, approached me, and asked, "Did you call for security?"

"Yes, officer. Thank you for getting here so quickly. I've just come from Dr. Schumacher's house on College Avenue."

He nodded.

"We were discussing . . . well, it doesn't matter. Things got a little heated, and . . . uh . . . I had to run out of house. He was very angry. He threatened me, and I was scared."

The officer's eyes bored into me. "He threatened you?"

"Yes."

"Dr. Jacob Schumacher?"

"Yes."

"When you say he threatened you . . ."

"He picked up the poker from the fireplace."

"And?"

"He came toward me."

"Do you have any reason to think he was going to hurt you?"

"Yes. He said he stopped my student from researching what she discovered in the mural in the chapel. He doesn't want . . ."

"Is it possible you're overreacting just a bit?"

"I saw the look in his eye. He was going to hit me."

The officer pulled out his cell phone. "Would you like me to call Dr. Schumacher and ask him what the problem is?"

"Of course not. He's not going to admit he was about to commit a crime."

"Well then I'm not sure what you expect me to do."

"I'm telling you he threatened me, and he practically admitted killing Kate Conrad."

"I see. I'm sure you understand campus security does not investigate major crimes. So, I'll pass this along to the appropriate authorities. You have a nice evening." He turned and walked back out to his cruiser.

I turned back to the circulation desk, and saw the woman with the glasses and the vest was looking at the student newspaper, and another woman, this one tall and thin with light brown hair and a long, straight nose, was pointing to something on the front page and whispering in her ear. As I approached, the first librarian glared at me.

"Excuse me," I said, "I need to reach Sheriff Mason Adams at the Edwards County Sheriff's Department. I'm sorry I don't have his phone number handy . . ."

"We're closing in about fifteen minutes, and we're a little busy right now," said the librarian with the glasses. Both of them turned and walked away.

I felt like I'd been punched. Apparently, the article about Kate's "lesbian affair" in the student newspaper was being fed into the campus gossip mill. It seemed people were turning against me, perhaps because the article called her my "favorite."

I walked out the front doors of the library. The late-afternoon light put a hard glare on everything. I felt more afraid than I ever had in my life. Where could I go? Jacob could be anywhere by now, waiting for me to show up.

I needed help, and, since my first day on this campus, Abbie had been the person to help me. To get to her place, I would have to walk by Jacob's house and turn on Ohio Avenue, which led back to Montgomery where the Rabbit Hutches were. That would be like inviting him to follow me to a semi-secluded location.

But I could also get to her place by running out to the athletic fields and circling back through the grove of birches to the far end of Montgomery Avenue. Jacob would have no reason to expect me to do that, and, though he could follow me in his car to the gymnasium, he would have no way to follow me once I got to the footpath through the birches.

I took off in that direction and found that the pumps I was wearing were lousy for running an extended distance. The one-inch heels, so comfortable for walking around campus, hammered my feet in a way I felt all the way up to my knees. As soon as I could, I got onto a lawn, took off my shoes, and carried one in each hand. I had to keep my eyes on the ground in front of me so I wouldn't trip on a tree root or a low spot in the turf, but I made good progress.

By the time I came within sight of the gymnasium, I felt good. My situation at the college may have morphed into a scene from a horror movie, but I felt at home when I was running. As long as I kept running, nothing could hurt me. Of course, that was not true, but it felt true, and that's what I needed at that moment.

When I got to the footpath that led through the birches to Montgomery Avenue, it occurred to me that Abbie might not be home. That didn't matter. I had nowhere else to go. If I got there and found her gone, I would lurk behind her Hutch, climb up on the roof, break in, or whatever. At least I would be someplace where Jacob would not come looking for me— probably.

When I came to the end of Montgomery Avenue, I saw her walk by the front window of her place. She was there. With a fresh burst of energy, I powered on until I stopped at her front door, out of breath.

She opened her door, and I pushed past her without saying anything. She closed the door and stood with her arms crossed. "And hello to you too."

"I need to call Sheriff Adams," I said, standing in the middle of her living-dining-kitchen room.

She drew breath as if to ask me something but shook it off and went into her bedroom for a moment. When she returned, she handed me her cell phone, sat at her pedestal table and opened her laptop. After a momentary search, she said, "Sheriff Mason Adams," and read out his phone number.

I punched in the numbers and got his voicemail. "Sheriff Adams? This is Nicole Noonan. I need to speak to you right away. It's urgent. Please call me at this number." Prompted by Abbie, I recited her phone number and hung up.

Chapter 35

Abbie gave me a skeptical look. "I believe the expression is, 'WTF?'"

"Jacob killed Kate, and he tried to kill me," I said, still out of breath.

Abbie stared at me for a moment before asking, "Why do you think Jacob killed Kate?"

I sat opposite her and put her phone on the table. "He said so."

"You were speaking with him? When? Where?"

"I've just come from his house. Well, not directly. I went to the library first . . . but that doesn't matter. I went to his house around three o'clock to talk about Kate's research on the mural. She had found this image. It's very small, way up in the corner, of a child with stab wounds. Historically, this image has been used to spread a lie about Jews murdering Christian children in a blood ritual. I told Jacob I knew he had tried to suppress her research, and he said, 'That's why I had to stop her.'"

Abbie thought about that for a moment. "He had to stop her. Did he say how?"

"He meant, 'That's why I killed her.'"

"How do you know that?"

"He picked up a poker from the fireplace and came at me with it."

"He tried to hit you with a poker?"

"I didn't give him a chance . . ."

Abbie's phone rang. She looked at it and handed it to me. I answered and heard a familiar baritone voice.

"Dr. Noonan? This is Sheriff Adams. What is it that's so urgent?"

"I know who . . . I mean, I have information about who killed Kate Conrad."

"Is this new information?"

"Yes. It just happened. I mean I just heard it."

"All right. If that's true, I would like to talk to you about that, but I have to ask, have you been questioning people about this case? Because I've warned you before . . ."

"No, Sheriff. This is nothing like that. I was pursuing my research, and something came up, and I had to run. I think I am in some danger. I have alerted the campus police, but I need to talk to you about this new evidence."

The sheriff was silent for a few seconds. "Would you like me to come to your office?"

"I can't . . . uh, no. I am at the home of another member of the faculty. We should speak here." I gave him Abbie's name and address.

"I'll be there as soon as I can. About twenty minutes."

We hung up, and I handed Abbie's phone back to her. She stood up and said, "I'm going to make us some tea. You just sit right there."

While she was busy at the stove and sink, I leaned back, closed my eyes and tried to calm down though it was hard to sit still. Images of Jacob, the librarians, and the campus police officer flashed through my mind. I had to open my eyes and look out the front windows just to make sure Jacob wasn't out there.

"Milk? Sweetener?" Abbie asked.

"Milk and sugar, if you have it."

She put two mugs of tea on the table and sat with me again. "You were saying he had a poker."

"Yes. Actually, first he said he told Kate to look into other possible meanings of this image, and she wouldn't listen to reason, which doesn't sound like Kate. Then he said, 'That's why I had to stop her.' As he said that, he picked up the poker from the fireplace and took a step toward me. From the look in his eyes, there was no doubt what he intended to do."

"But he did not take another step toward you or try to hit you with the poker?"

"When I saw him coming I picked up a book from the coffee table in front of me and threw it at that cabinet in the corner, the one with the glass front where he has the porcelain. While he was distracted, I ran out the front door."

"So it's not clear what he would have done if you hadn't distracted him?"

"If I had waited for it to get any clearer, I'd be dead. My brains would be all over the floor of Jacob's living room." That came out louder than I wanted it to.

"Nicole, I'm on your side. I'm just trying to anticipate what the sheriff might say. I suggest you think about how you want to put this to him."

"You're right." I sipped some tea and took deep breaths.

"You don't want this to sound like you had a disagreement with Jacob and got so upset you started throwing things. Let's keep it simple. On the phone, you told the sheriff you have information about the murder."

"Yes. Jacob confessed to killing Kate."

"That might sound like you're jumping to a conclusion. You were talking with him about Kate's research, and he said . . . what?"

"He said, 'That's why I had to stop her.'"

Abbie frowned and stared out the window for a moment. "That's a little vague. What if he said, 'That's why I got rid of her?'"

"But he didn't say that."

"But, maybe that's what you heard."

"You're suggesting I lie to the sheriff?"

"Do you want him to question Jacob? If so, then give him a reason to do it. You've had a terrifying experience. You can't be sure what you heard. That's how you remember it."

"Okay. He said, 'That's why I got rid of her.'"

"Hold on." Abbie got up and went to the front window to look out at Montgomery Avenue. "The campus cop has arrived. He's just sitting there in his cruiser."

"The sheriff probably called him."

Abbie sat again and looked me in the eye. "Are you okay? Just focus. Of course, you're upset. It was a scary experience. Let him see that. Tell him why he should go and question Jacob."

I nodded. "I get it. Unfortunately, I also left my purse there. I was so terrified I ran out without thinking about it. That's why I turned up here without calling first."

"Don't worry about that now. Just focus on getting the sheriff to question Jacob about how he threatened you."

"Okay. Right."

Abbie went to the window again. "Okay. The sheriff's here. He's coming to the door. His deputy is out there chatting with the campus cop."

We heard a knock, and Abbie opened the door. "Good afternoon, Sheriff. Please come in."

Adams stepped over the threshold and glanced around. In the crowded room, he looked even bigger than usual.

Abbie waved him toward a chair by the front window and said, "Nicole wants to talk to you. If you'll excuse me, I'll be in the other room." She went into the bedroom and closed the door.

Adams put his hat on one of the easy chairs, sat on the other, and took out his notebook. When he looked up at me, his expression softened a bit. I think he could see I was scared. "You have some information for me?"

"Yes, Sheriff. This afternoon—over an hour ago, now—I went to the home of Professor Jacob Schumacher to discuss the work of my student, Kate Conrad. He advised her on her research. When I mentioned that she had discovered an image in the mural on the wall of the chapel—something that could be embarrassing to the college—he said, 'That's why I had to get rid of her.'"

"Those were his words?"

"That's what I remember."

He made a note. "And what time was this?"

"I got to his house at three o'clock. I don't know how long we talked. When he said that, he picked up the poker from the fireplace and walked toward me. I got scared and ran out."

Adams made another note. "You said this image is embarrassing?"

"It's a picture of a child who has died from being stabbed many times. This idea has an evil history going back hundreds of years. It's used to illustrate false accusations about Jews killing children."

Adams looked up from his pad and stared at me wide-eyed. I am sure that in his many years of law enforcement, and probably in the military before that, he had seen a lot of evil things, but apparently he hadn't seen or heard of this one. "You said you were afraid. Did he threaten you or try to hit you with the poker?"

"I didn't stay around to find out."

Adams nodded and finished his note-taking. "Are you willing to sign a statement to this effect, giving all the details of this event?"

"Yes. Absolutely."

He put away his notebook and stood up. "All right. Thank you, Dr. Noonan." He picked up his hat.

"Are you going to arrest him?"

"I'll speak to him."

"Sheriff, I'm afraid to go back to my home. I don't think I'm safe on campus with him here."

"I'm going to speak with him right now. I'll let you know whether you should take any special precautions."

Given the situation, I decided to see whether having "doctor" in front of my name would get me any special privileges. I sidestepped to put myself between him and the door. "I want to go with you."

"That won't be necessary."

"I want to be there when you speak to him."

"That's not how we do things."

I remembered what Abbie said about my purse, but I needed a reason to go with him and confront Jacob. "The thing is, Sheriff, I was so afraid that I ran out of his house and left my purse behind. I have to go back and get it, but I can't go back by myself."

He took time to inhale and let it out slowly. "All right then." He glanced at the bedroom door. "We should let your friend know we're leaving."

I knocked on the door. Abbie opened it and joined us.

"Thank you, ma'am," said Adams. "We'll be on our way now."

"You're welcome, Sheriff."

Adams left. On the way out the door, I looked back at Abbie. She gave me a thumbs up.

Chapter 36

When the sheriff's cruiser stopped on College Avenue in front of Jacob's house, I had a sinking feeling that he wouldn't be there. I could be stuck without my keys, phone, and wallet. I started to panic, so I focused on the present. I was in a sheriff's cruiser with two officers who were taking my story seriously. This was a huge improvement over my situation when I ran out of Jacob's house an hour ago. Things were going well, and they would continue to get better. I had to keep telling myself that.

When the sheriff and his deputy got out of the car, I tried to do the same. "Hey! My door won't open."

The deputy opened my door from the outside. As I got out, he said, "Ma'am, I suggest you wait for us in the car."

"I'm coming in with you."

"It's for your own safety, ma'am."

"I have to get my purse," I said too loudly.

The deputy looked to Adams, who rested his eyes on me. He couldn't help looking down on me because of his height, but it seemed he was no longer looking down on me as an inferior person.

He turned to the deputy and said, "It's okay. She might be able to help."

It wasn't the most lavish compliment I'd ever received, but it made me feel better than anything I'd heard in a long time. The deputy nodded and waved for me to follow the sheriff up the front walk to the house.

When we got to the front door, Adams paused before ringing the bell. "One word, and my deputy will escort you out."

I nodded.

He rang the bell.

It took Jacob only a few seconds to answer the door. "Good afternoon, Sheriff. Oh, Nicole, you left this when you were here earlier." He picked up my purse from a cabinet by the door and handed it to me.

I was glad to have it back in my hands, but it was unnerving how Jacob made it sound like we'd had a normal, social visit.

Adams asked, "Dr. Schumacher, may we come in and speak with you for a few minutes?"

"Of course." He stepped back and waved us in. "Let's sit in here," he said, pointing the way through the archway to the living room.

I took the armchair furthest from the door. The sheriff took the love seat, and Jacob sat in his usual armchair with his back to the archway and clasped his hands over his belly. The deputy sat behind me in a chair by the windows.

I glanced at the fireplace. The poker hung in its usual place alongside the other tools. Seeing it made me shiver. The book I had thrown was back in its place on the table, and the display case in the corner was intact, as I expected. I was glad to have Adams between the professor and me.

Adams had his notebook out. "Professor, were you acquainted with the student who is recently deceased, Kate Conrad?"

Jacob sighed. "Yes, I was. It's very sad."

"Was she a student in one of your classes?"

"No. I met her earlier this semester."

"Under what circumstances did you meet her?"

Jacob smiled while still seeming to feel sad. It was an impressive performance. "I think Nicole could tell you better than I could."

The sheriff said, "I'd like to hear it from you."

Jacob's eyes searched the far wall of the room as if he could see the past illustrated there. "I dropped over to the chapel one afternoon when Nicole was there studying the mural. She has been generous about sharing her research with me. Her student happened to be there with her."

"Was this the first time you met Kate Conrad?"

"I believe it was, yes."

"And when was this?"

"I can't recall. It was shortly before we heard the news of her death. Do you recall, Nicole?"

Adams ignored the question and forged ahead. "Was this the only time you spoke with her?"

"No. I think we spoke in passing one other time."

I crossed my arms and held on tight so I wouldn't blurt out that he had spoken to Kate at the library the next day, the day she died.

Adams glanced at his notebook before asking, "Professor, were you aware of the nature of Kate Conrad's research?"

At this, Jacob showed the first genuine surprise I had seen since we arrived. He also seemed irritated. "As I said, I met her in the chapel with Nicole, so I assume she was studying the mural."

Adams turned to me. "Is that correct, Dr. Noonan?"

Apparently the one-word rule had been lifted. "Yes, and Dr. Schumacher knows that very well since he called Kate's parents after she died and asked them to send her notebook to him."

Adams turned to Schumacher. "Is this true, Doctor?"

Jacob smiled and looked at me. "That's right. You were supposed to come by and pick that up last week, weren't you, Nicole? If you like, I can get it for you now."

I was ready to demand that he explain how I was supposed to pick it up when he had gone behind my back to get it, but before I could speak, Adams asked Jacob, "Where were you on the evening when Kate Conrad was killed?"

If Adams had smacked his face, Jacob could not have looked more surprised, but he recovered quickly and seemed to shrug off the question. "I was at home." He chuckled. "I don't have an alibi. Do I need one?"

"Professor, I think it would be a good idea to get that notebook now. Where is it?"

"Upstairs, in my study," said Jacob, already halfway out of his chair.

"Deputy Harding will go with you."

Jacob froze, standing in front of his chair. "I don't see why that's necessary—to be followed by an officer in my own home."

Adams sounded apologetic as he said, "It's a protocol we're required to follow."

Jacob hesitated, glancing back and forth between Adams and me. "Very well then," he said.

Jacob went through the archway, across the foyer, and up the stairs. The deputy was a few steps behind him all the way.

When they were out of sight, Adams leaned toward me and spoke softly. "He's not going to confess. I'm not sure how much more we can accomplish here."

I pointed toward the fireplace. "Take the poker. It's evidence."

Adams shook his head. "Of what? It's not the murder weapon. From examining the wound, the medical examiner says she was struck by something about two inches wide with a flat surface. That poker is round."

Having never thought about the exact nature of Kate's wound, I felt a bit queasy. "Can we search the house?"

"He wouldn't still have the weapon here."

"He might, and if he does, he'll certainly get rid of it after this visit. This might be our only chance."

Adams mulled that for a moment and said, "I'll see what I can do."

We heard footsteps on the stairway. Adams studied his notebook and I let my eyes scan the items on the mantle.

"Here you are," said Jacob with a smile as he set the notebook on the coffee table between us.

I was jolted by the sight of such an ordinary object—a spiral-bound notebook with a student's doodles on the cover—endowed with such importance by the events of recent weeks.

"Well then, if there's nothing else . . ." said Jacob as he stood by his chair.

Adams rose from the sofa. It was like watching a bear go up on its hind legs. "With your permission, Professor, we would like to walk through the house."

I'll admit I enjoyed watching Jacob's mask of humor and detachment slide from Jacob's face.

"For what purpose?"

"It would help us eliminate you as a suspect."

Jacob could no longer pretend to take all this lightly. "Oh! I'm a suspect now?" There was resentment in his tone.

"Everyone is a suspect until we bring charges against someone. We just want to look through the house so we can report there is nothing here to connect you to the crime."

"Excuse me, Sheriff, but I believe you need a search warrant to do that."

"We'll get one if you prefer, but if we can do this now we won't have to come back and bother you later this evening. Also, this way there won't be anything on record about getting a warrant to search your house."

Adams won the staring contest. Jacob said, "All right, but please be careful. I don't want anything disturbed or broken."

"What's through here?" asked Adams as he walked toward the archway that lead to the dining room. Jacob followed him.

Chapter 37

Deputy Harding gestured for me to join him. "Stay with me," he said as we went into the kitchen of Jacob's house.

Harding opened the broom closet and went on to open cabinets and drawers. I was surprised at how little Jacob had in his kitchen. Obviously, he didn't spend much time there.

After a few minutes, I heard Jacob's voice from the next room. "Where are the others?" A moment later he came through the swinging door that separated the kitchen and dining room. He glared at the deputy. "What are you doing in here?"

"We have to look at everything," said Harding.

"No. I want to be present when you are searching. I want everyone in one room."

Adams appeared behind him. "Professor, if we do it that way, we're going to be here a very long time. Deputy Harding is a professional. He's trained. He will leave everything as he found it. If he has questions, he will speak to you and me immediately."

Jacob seemed on the verge of exploding as he pointed at me. "She has no right to search my belongings."

"I'm here to make sure she does not touch anything," said Harding. He looked at me. "You understand that, don't you?"

I folded my arms and nodded.

"Is there a closet by the front door?" asked Adams.

Jacob marched through the kitchen to the foyer. Adams followed.

Harding finished in the kitchen, and we walked out to the foyer just in time to hear Adams ask, "How many rooms are upstairs?"

"Three, plus the bathroom," said Jacob.

We all went up and followed the same method. The sheriff went with Jacob into the bedroom; Harding and I went into the guest room. The closet there was empty as were most of the drawers. The bed, dresser, chair, and nightstand had the look of furniture bought second hand to furnish this room. It seemed Jacob had done just enough to make it look like a guest room without going to the expense and bother of making it comfortable for a guest.

Harding and I finished and waited in the hallway outside the bedroom door. Jacob's own room was luxurious by comparison with a leather club chair by the window, art on the walls, and a fine carpet between the bed and dresser.

When the sheriff and Jacob came out and went into the study, Harding and I looked into the bathroom and the linen closet. Again, we found only bare necessities.

I might have felt sorry for Jacob while this search went on, but whenever I remembered we were looking for an object with a flat surface heavy enough to cause fatal brain damage my sympathy evaporated.

Again, I waited with the deputy in the hall and peeked through the doorway while Adams and Jacob finished their search of the study, which contained the book collection of a man who knew he would never have to move to another home. It covered two walls of the room and included many fine bindings.

Adams called the deputy into the room, and together they pulled out a few books on each shelf to make sure there was nothing hidden behind them. Jacob sat on the small sofa across the room, barely able to keep still, he was so upset by this invasion of privacy. While Adams finished the bookshelves, Harding looked into the closet and looked under each piece of furniture as he had in the guest room.

They proceeded downstairs without a word and I followed. When we were all in the foyer, Adams asked, "Is there a basement?" Without replying, Jacob turned and led us through the kitchen to a door that opened onto a wooden stairway. He switched on a light and went down followed by Adams and Harding. At the doorway, I paused to get used to a musty smell rising from below and to let my eyes adjust to the darkness.

When I got to the foot of the stairs, I saw Harding already at the far end of the room using his flashlight to look under a fuel-storage tank and heater. Adams was inspecting a workbench on the right side of the room. Jacob stood by some pieces of luggage and file boxes stacked haphazardly in the center of the floor. A set of wooden shelving covered about half of the left wall. The shelves had nothing on them.

The foundation walls of the house were made of stone fitted with mortar, and the concrete floor was dusty. Narrow windows, three on each side, let some daylight in, and a bare light bulb burned in the middle of the ceiling.

I stopped near the workbench since it seemed to be the most likely place to find a murder weapon. Apparently, Jacob had little use for it. The rack held only a few screwdrivers, pliers, and a hammer. On the work surface, two new paintbrushes were laid out along with a new can of paint. On the shelf below were several old paint cans. A stepladder leaned against the wall next to it. I couldn't see anything with a flat surface that could be used to inflict a blow. Nonetheless, Adams used his flashlight to go over everything.

After looking at the items stacked in the middle of the room, Harding waited at the foot of the stairs.

Adams finished at the workbench and looked to Harding, who shook his head. "Thank you, Professor," said the sheriff.

Jacob wasted no time crossing the room and climbing the stairs. Harding followed. Adams waved for me to go next, and I went up, all the while wishing I could think of some excuse to stay and keep looking. I couldn't think of any place that hadn't been checked, but I didn't want to give up on finding something that would prove Jacob murdered Kate.

When I got to the top of the stairs, I saw that Jacob and Harding had already gone through to the foyer. Adams came up after me, and I stopped in the middle of the kitchen to speak to him. "Sheriff, we have to check one more thing."

He looked pained, but he waited to hear what I had to say.

"Those shelves in the basement are new. The wood is bare, and there's a new can of paint on the workbench."

Adams nodded. "I saw that."

"On Tuesday of this week, I saw Huey Littleton loading some lumber into his truck in front of this house."

"The professor probably hired him to build some shelving in the basement."

"There's one other thing we should check. Will you lend me your flashlight?"

Jacob's voice sounded from the foyer. "Sheriff, please! This has gone on long enough."

"I think we're finished here," Adams said to me.

"This will just take a minute. We have to look now. This could be our last chance."

Adams frowned, but he called out to the foyer, "We just need to look at one more thing." He handed me his flashlight and followed me back down the stairs.

The shelving was built of two-by-four lumber and plywood. It stood about as tall as I do, which left space on top to store things. I set up the stepladder and looked at the top of the new shelving. The entire surface was unmarked.

I got off the stepladder and shone the flashlight on the underside of the top shelves, giving special attention to the two-by-four cross braces, which were about as long as my arm. Here too, all the lumber looked fresh and new.

The result was the same when I inspected the top and underside of the middle shelf, which was a little above my waist. That left the bottom shelf, which was about six inches off the floor. I looked around for a drop cloth or some old towels or bedding to protect the blazer and slacks I wore for the classroom, but saw nothing.

Footsteps sounded on the kitchen floor above. Jacob's voice came from the top of the stairs. "Sheriff, please! I must insist."

I got down on my belly and turned my head on the side to look under the bottom shelf. There, on the cross brace in the center, was a brownish stain smaller than a dime. In the glare from the flashlight, I could see three or four hairs attached to it.

I pushed up, got my knees under me, and held out the flashlight. "I think you'd better see this, Sheriff. It's on the cross brace toward the back. It's faint, but you can see it with the flashlight."

He took the flashlight from me and said, "Stand over there please." He pointed to the workbench across the room.

I backed away and watched as he grabbed the middle shelf with both hands, slid the entire set of shelving away from the wall, and tipped it back so he could look under it more easily. Crouching on one knee, he bent forward and shone his light on the underside of the bottom shelf.

Jacob came halfway down the stairs and yelled, "What are you doing?"

Adams ignored him.

"Sheriff!" Jacob roared.

Harding appeared above him on the stairs and said, "Let's wait right here, Professor."

No one moved as Adams studied the shelving for several seconds before rising and announcing, "This is now an active crime scene. Professor, please wait upstairs with Deputy Harding. Dr. Noonan, please wait in the kitchen."

Chapter 38

"What are you talking about? I demand an explanation," yelled Jacob.

Harding put a hand on his arm and urged him upstairs to the kitchen. I waited until they were out of sight before following them up. Adams remained on one knee in the basement, studying the cross brace and talking into his cell phone.

I felt awkward standing around by myself in Jacob's kitchen, wondering what would happen next. Jacob and Harding must have gone into the living room because they weren't in the foyer. I couldn't hear them speaking, but I could hear the sheriff's voice from downstairs. The house was so quiet I became aware of my own footsteps and stopped pacing the kitchen floor.

After about five minutes the sheriff came upstairs and nodded to me as he walked through into the foyer. I wasn't sure what he was confirming, but I was glad to receive a yes rather than a no. I followed him into the foyer and stood by the archway as he went into the living room and sat on the sofa, facing the fireplace as he had before. Jacob sat as usual in the armchair with his back to the foyer, and Harding occupied the facing armchair where I had sat before. I made myself as inconspicuous as possible.

Adams spoke in a business-like manner. "Professor, I have found what I believe to be traces of blood and hair on the underside of the wooden shelving in your basement. This is why I have declared your basement an active crime scene. I have ordered a team of forensic technicians to come here and process the scene. It will probably take more than an hour for them to arrive. I will remain here to meet them. In the meantime, what can you tell me about how blood and hair, if that's what they are, came to be on your shelving?"

I could see only the back of Jacob's head. He seemed to sit absolutely still as he spoke. "I hired Huey Littleton to build that shelving. He delivered all the lumber over a month ago. For a while it just sat in the basement because he was busy with work elsewhere. He would come by for a few hours each weekend to work on the project. One evening this week he picked up the remaining lumber because he had finished building the shelves. He is supposed to come back next weekend and paint them. I'm not sure what else I can tell you."

Adams made a few notes before saying, "So you did not at any time inspect the lumber or handle it in any way?"

Jacob shook his head. "I had no reason to. It was just lumber. I rarely go down to the basement. I recently decided to put some shelves down there because my study had become overcrowded. I boxed up some old papers and needed to put the boxes somewhere. I didn't want to set them on the floor because of the dampness."

Again, Adams made some notes. "Professor, if I'm correct, and the technicians confirm that there are traces of blood and hair on one of the two-by-fours, we will compare the DNA evidence with test results from the remains of Kate Conrad to see if they match. If they do, there will be a strong presumption that a piece of lumber used to build shelves in your basement was used as the murder weapon."

Jacob's head bent forward. "That's a horrible thought. It makes me sick to think Huey could have done something like that. The idea that he would leave the actual piece of wood he used in my basement . . . I can't even think about this."

"Professor, let me suggest the following. What you've just told me is information critical to our investigation. We need to get this in a signed statement while it is still fresh in your mind.

"When the forensic team arrives, it's going to get very noisy and very busy here for a while: floodlights set up, people going in and out. I think it would be best if you went with Deputy Harding to the Sheriff's Department's office so he can take down your statement. Of course, he will bring you back when that's done.

" By then, the team should be finished here. I will be on hand to keep the place secure while they are here and until you return. Would you be willing to do that to help us in our investigation?"

Jacob hesitated before saying, "If you think it will help."

Harding rose and came out to the foyer to wait by the front door. Jacob followed him and got his jacket from the closet. Harding walked out the door to the cruiser.

As Jacob approached the door, he stepped close enough to me so that he could speak softly. His eyes were heavy lidded. "This is too bad. I had hope for you as a colleague."

I stared him down. "You are a failure as a teacher, as a scholar, and as a human being."

Without reacting, he turned and walked out into the night.

I went into the living room and sat in the far chair to talk to the sheriff. "You can't let him blame this on Huey Littleton. I heard Schumacher say, 'That's why I had to get rid of her.'"

Without taking his eyes from his notebook, he said, "I'm aware of what you told me and of what Professor Schumacher said. I am continuing to investigate."

I leaned forward, and spoke louder. "Even if it turns out that Huey brought that piece of lumber into the house with the blood and hair on it, it's still possible Jacob hired him to kill her, and he'd still be guilty as an accomplice or something, wouldn't he?"

Adams sat back and looked at me with patience and perhaps a note of amusement. "Dr. Noonan, this is not my first investigation."

I must have been blushing because my face felt hot. "I'm sorry. I shouldn't try to tell you how to do your job."

"I appreciate that," said Adams, and he smiled.

"Is it really going to get noisy and chaotic when the technicians arrive?"

"I might have exaggerated a bit to get the professor to go to the office without having to arrest him."

So, Adams had something in the works. "May I stay and watch what the technicians do? I've never seen what happens at a crime scene."

"It's time for you to go home, Dr. Noonan."

I felt a chill at the thought of returning to my Rabbit Hutch—walking back in the dark, the sparse furnishings, the loneliness.

As if reading my thoughts, Adams said, "We have Huey Littleton locked up, and, just between you and me, I don't think Professor Schumacher will be returning to campus this evening."

"Thank you, Sheriff. That's good to know."

Adams nodded. "I'll call you this weekend to let you know what's happening."

I thanked him, picked up my purse and Kate's notebook, and left.

The walk from Jacob's house to my Hutch took less than ten minutes, but it felt like a four-hour hike. I hadn't been home since going to Jacob's house at three, and that seemed like a week ago.

I dropped my purse and Kate's notebook on the cafe table and went into the bedroom. When I saw myself in the long mirror, I didn't know whether to laugh or cry. My blazer and slacks looked like they'd been used to sweep a floor, which is essentially what happened in Jacob's basement. I took them off and put them into a plastic shopping bag to go to the dry cleaner in Blanton.

I took a hot shower. I needed a bath to provide heat deep in my joints, but the Rabbit Hutches are equipped with a shower stall only. I put on boxers, a t-shirt, sweats, and slippers.

I wandered from my bedroom to the living-dining-kitchen room, not knowing what I would do next. Kate's notebook caught my eye. I picked it up from my cafe table, sat in one of my beach chairs, and opened it.

Her handwriting was precise. She had skipped a line on the page whenever she wanted to separate one thought from another. She had indented a paragraph when she wanted to indicate she was paraphrasing rather than recording her own thoughts.

I got a bit teary as I scanned her notes from the two weeks of art history class she had attended. I remembered saying the things she had summarized on the pages in front of me. These notes were a record of the precious few hours when we had been thinking the same thing at the same time.

After a dozen pages, the notebook was blank. I flipped forward and found another series of pages on which she had taken notes directly from the textbook. I scanned them and saw she had been several chapters ahead of the syllabus. She was that rare and wonderful student who was driven by her own curiosity rather than a teacher's instructions.

Following another blank section, I found her notes on the mural. After a series of descriptive paragraphs, I saw notes on her discovery of the coffins in the treetop and the stabbed child. Her study ended with two pages of bibliographic citations. She had relentlessly stalked the meaning of that image, and had found it, not as I had by stumbling upon *Dark Mirror,* but through a series of articles in scholarly journals. She was a true scholar. She had a nose for finding the truth.

I set her notebook aside and juggled competing feelings of gratitude and loss. I was grateful to have had such an intellectual soulmate even for a short time. I doubted I would have another one anytime soon.

My meditation was interrupted by a more basic sensation. I'd barely eaten all day. I looked in the miniature fridge and found I didn't even have enough for a good stir-fry.

My phone rang. It was Abbie. I dropped into one of my beach chairs.

"Looks like you're home. How did it go?" she asked.

"Do you have food?"

"That's what I like about you, Noonan. I never have to guess what's on your mind. Let me see . . . hmm . . . I have eggs, cheese, yogurt . . ."

"Oh my god! Breakfast! You're lucky I'm too weak to lift myself out of this beach chair. Otherwise I would come over there and steal the contents of your refrigerator."

"All right: breakfast for dinner. I'll be over in five minutes."

Chapter 39

While waiting for Abbie to arrive with ingredients for a meal, I lapsed into a semi-conscious state in which I reviewed the events of the last several hours. Jacob and I had sat talking about the mural, Kate's research, the Enlightenment, anti-Semitism, and how he wanted to explain that image of a murdered child in the context of the life and times of Felix Fuchs. He had said Kate wouldn't listen to reason, and he'd had to stop her. Then he'd picked up that poker, and for a second it looked like getting tenure was the least of my worries.

I heard a knock at my door, answered it, and there was Abbie with a grocery bag. "You look like something the cat dragged in," she said.

"That's exactly how I feel."

She unloaded her bag on what passed for a kitchen counter, and I flopped back in my beach chair.

"So, what happened after you left my place with the sheriff?" she asked.

"We rode over to Jacob's house, and I talked Adams into letting me come in with him."

"That was smart."

"Thanks. He asked Jacob how he knew Kate, and—I can hardly believe it even now—Jacob made up this alternate reality, starting with, 'Oh, Nicole, you left your purse when you were here earlier.' Also, according to him, I was supposed to pick up Kate's notebook from him last week."

"Couldn't you blow the whistle on any of this?"

"Adams had me under a gag order."

Abbie brought a glass of beer over and set it on the table next to my beach chair. "Go easy with that. I don't want you to pass out before the eggs are ready."

I took a sip. Beer never tasted better.

I continued with my story. "What happened next really surprised me. He sent Jacob upstairs to get the notebook and asked me what I thought we should do. I said we should search the house for the murder weapon, we did, and we found it."

Abbie stopped mixing the eggs. "You found the murder weapon? What was it?"

"A two-by-four."

"How do you know it was the murder weapon?"

"It had blood and hair on it."

"And Jacob just left it lying around his house?"

"Not exactly. Huey Littleton had used it to build some shelves in Jacob's basement."

Abbie stared at me for a moment, shook her head, and said, "This is getting too weird." She finished beating the eggs and poured them into the skillet.

"I still don't understand exactly what happened. I know Jacob killed her because I heard him say he had to stop her, but otherwise it would seem possible that Huey killed her and then hid the two-by-four by using it in Jacob's shelving."

Abbie dished up two plates and put them on the cafe table along with a jar of marmalade for the toast. I brought my glass of beer to the table, sat down, and took a bite of the eggs, put some marmalade on the toast, took a bite of it, and took a swallow of beer.

"So I guess it tastes okay?" Abbie gave me her best ironic smile.

"I cannot begin to describe how good this tastes. You are saving my life."

Feeling no shame, I kept eating until I had finished the eggs.

Sitting back with a piece of toast and half a glass of beer I said, "I think it's just hitting me that he actually killed someone in order to stop her from writing about something he wanted to keep secret. I know that's what happened, but I still can't believe it. How could it be so important to him to control that information?"

Abbie paused with a forkful of eggs. "It's the reputation of his ancestors. It's the history of the place where he lives and works. He has made it the subject of his research. It's everything to him."

"True, and, judging by the way he coughs up blood every now and then, he doesn't have long to finish his biography of Fuchs."

Abbie nodded. "I'm not sure what's wrong with him. I heard he's been going up to Ohio State for treatments. I don't know what his outlook is." She finished her beer. "Do you think he still might get away with it?"

I was starting to feel a bit drowsy. "Adams told me he didn't think Jacob would be returning to campus this weekend, so he must have something in the works, but I don't know what it is. I don't see how he can prove Jacob used that two-by-four. Also, I don't see how Jacob could have met Kate at that spot where the path across the field meets the road."

She took the dishes to the sink and started washing. When I got up to help her, she said, "Sit down. Let me do this for you." I was happy to oblige.

Over the clatter of the dishes and the hiss of running water, she said, "Assuming Adams arrests him, Jacob will have to appear in court. The prosecution will try to persuade the court to deny bail. I'm not sure how all that works."

"I think I'd better stay in touch with Adams this weekend," I replied. "Come to think of it, he said I would have to come to his office and sign a statement. Maybe I can go there tomorrow."

I tried to think how that might work if Lionel and I were going to have our dinner date tomorrow evening. I didn't even know where the sheriff's office was. If it was in the direction of Columbus, maybe we could stop on our way. Nothing says romance like cooperating with law enforcement.

Abbie dried her hands and sat down opposite me. "I want to make sure you'll be okay this weekend because I'm heading to Pittsburgh tomorrow morning."

Despite my grief and fatigue I had to smile at that. "Are you really? And will you be seeing a certain someone?"

She nodded. "That's the plan. In fact, I hope I'll be doing a lot more than just seeing her. Anyway, I'm staying over tomorrow night and coming back Sunday evening."

"Good for you."

"What are your plans?"

"Lionel and I are having dinner. We'll probably drive up to Columbus."

"Still taking it slow with him?"

"I'm not sure where we're headed."

"I hope that works out for you."

"We'll see."

Lionel was very accommodating about stopping at the sheriff's office on our way to Columbus so I could sign a statement. He even joked about it, saying it would give him a chance to see if all the deputies would pull their weapons when a black man walked in the door. I failed to see the humor in that.

Over dinner at a favorite place of Lionel's in the Short North, I asked, "Have you heard anything from Northwestern?"

He shook his head.

"I'm sorry."

He shrugged. "That doesn't mean anything. I'd be surprised if they made a decision before December."

I took a sip of wine. "For your sake, I hope they offer you the job."

"Thank you, although in a way I hope they don't."

"Thank you."

We took some time to enjoy our food.

"Here's an idea," I said. "If they offer you the job, tell them you'll accept it only if they also offer me a job in the art department."

He grinned. "I like that idea. It's not unheard of, but I think they do that only for deans, vice presidents, and football coaches."

"Oh, I'm sorry," I said with heavy irony. "I thought you were applying to be the football coach."

He laughed. "No, they already turned me down for that, so I thought I'd try for French professor."

After another sip of wine, I said, "December is still a couple of months away."

"That's true," he said, "and there's no guarantee I'll know anything by then."

"So what should we do?"

"We could just take it slow."

"Yes," I said, "we could take it slow, but not too slow."

He smiled, reached across the table, and squeezed my hand.

Chapter 40

At about three thirty on Sunday afternoon, I strolled over to the Arts and Humanities Building to meet Sheriff Adams at my office. My day-off outfit of a sweater, jeans, and sneakers was now augmented with a t-shirt under the sweater and a windbreaker. Autumn in Ohio was as cold as any season ever got in San Francisco. Next weekend, I would have to set aside a day to go shopping for some real winter clothes.

The view from my office window over the wooded hillside was marvelous. Lionel had told me the fall color would be at its best this week, and it did not disappoint. I had seen paintings and photographs of autumn scenes in hardwood forests, but I had never seen the real thing. Orange was the dominant color, and there were gold accents. In the afternoon sunlight, the hillside looked as if it were on fire.

I heard a knock and turned around to see Sheriff Adams framed in the doorway. I remembered how impressed I'd been the first time I saw him there. I'd seen him many times since, but he was still impressive.

"Good afternoon, Sheriff. Have a seat."

"Good afternoon, Dr. Noonan."

As he sat, I held out my hand to take his hat. He gave it to me, and I set it on the corner of my desk, nearest him.

"How goes the investigation?"

"We had some long hours, Friday night into Saturday, but by yesterday afternoon we were able to send the case to the prosecutor."

This gave me a jolt of adrenaline.

He went on. "You may recall that when I questioned Huey Littleton regarding his whereabouts on the night of the murder he admitted he saw Kate Conrad at Buddy's Bar—he couldn't really deny it, because we had so many witnesses—but he claimed he didn't know anything about what happened after she left.

"When I told him we'd found the murder weapon, and that it was part of the shelving he'd built in Schumacher's basement, he started to look worried. Then I told him we knew he had a motive to kill her because everyone at Buddy's saw how angry he was, he had the means to kill her because he would have had a two-by-four in the back of his truck, and he had opportunity because he could have followed her after she left Buddy's.

"That's when he decided maybe he did have a little more to tell us. He said he was working at Schumacher's house on the Friday afternoon before she died. Before he left, the professor showed him a picture of a student and asked him to keep an eye out for her whenever he was in Blanton. He said the professor asked him to call right away whenever he saw her.

"So I asked him: If that's true where's the photo? He said it was probably still in his truck. We sent a deputy out, and sure enough it was on the floor under the driver's seat."

I held up a hand to stop the sheriff. "Wait a minute. Jacob had a photo of Kate?"

Adams nodded. "It looked like something that was printed from a computer. The prosecutor was glad to have that piece of evidence. He said it proves premeditation."

I knew this was good news for solving the murder, but it was also further evidence of the evil nature of a man I had thought of as a colleague. "So that night, outside Buddy's Bar, Huey recognized Kate as the student Jacob wanted him to spy on?" I asked.

Adams nodded. "That's right, and he admitted he saw her

after she left Buddy's. He said he drove around town and caught sight of her walking along Main Street and turning onto that path that crosses a field and comes out on route 212 where it leads to the campus. That's when he called Schumacher and told him her whereabouts."

"So Huey Littleton helped Jacob kill Kate?"

"Littleton says the professor never told him why he wanted to find her, and he never asked. I imagine that's true. I can't see why the professor would have shared that information.

"By the way, Littleton also confessed to vandalizing your car, though he swears Schumacher paid him to do it."

I'd already figured out Littleton did the spray-painting, so that didn't surprise me, but learning that Jacob had paid for it made my guts twist. Jacob must have seen me working in the chapel on that weekend before I met my class there. He could have watched me from his house across the street. I tried not to dwell on it. "So, based on Huey's testimony, you charged Jacob with murder?"

"There's a little more to it. Deputy Harding took his time processing Schumacher's statement Friday evening. You know how it is when you have computer problems." Adams smiled as he said this. "So, Schumacher was still in our office when we'd gotten all this out of Littleton. I took the professor into an interview room, told him I was arresting him on suspicion of murder, and read him his rights. Of course, he had to have a lawyer. That's when we knew we were in for a long night.

"Once the lawyer was there, I laid it out. We had proof of premeditation with the photo. He had means because he could have borrowed the two-by-four from the stack of lumber in his basement. He had motive because of what you told us about his opinion of Ms. Conrad's research. And he had opportunity because of what Littleton told us.

"Schumacher answered a few questions, but his lawyer shut it down pretty quick. Eventually everybody got some sleep, Schumacher spent the night in a cell, and we were back at it Saturday morning. When we got your statement, we called in the prosecutor. It's all up to the lawyers now. I'm not sure, but I think the professor is going to cooperate and plead guilty in return for a guarantee that the prosecutor won't seek the death penalty."

My chest felt hollow, and I had to take a deep breath before I could speak again. "There's something I'm still trying to make sense of. Jacob knew Kate was walking on that path because of Huey's phone call, and he would have had a rough idea of when she would reach route 212."

Adams nodded his agreement.

I continued. "So he could have driven down the road from campus, turned around, and been there waiting for her when she got to the end of the path and started walking along the road toward campus. But, at that point, if he had chased her in his car, she would have run into the woods, and if he had chased her on foot, she easily could have outrun him."

Adams scowled as if he hated what he was about to say. "Once his lawyer gave him the go-ahead to make a full confession, Schumacher admitted he stopped his car across the road from where Ms. Conrad was walking. According to his description, he then stepped out of the car, waved to her, and offered her a ride. When she crossed the road and started to walk in front of the car, he stepped behind her and hit her."

"And he left her lying there by the road," I said.

Adams nodded.

I felt cold all over wondering if Kate had a moment of terror as she saw a friendly gesture turn into violence.

"How did the two-by-four end up as part of his shelving?" I asked.

"I asked him about that. He said when he got home he went to the basement and threw it back on the pile of lumber, assuming it would get hauled away along with the rest of the scraps. I think it was by chance Littleton used to build the shelving. If he hadn't, I doubt we ever would have found it."

I could think of nothing else to say, and I had nothing to

ask. "Thank you for taking time to come here and go over this with me."

"You're welcome." Adams leaned forward and picked up his hat. "If there's nothing else, I'll be on my way."

"Sheriff, I want to apologize. From the beginning, I felt like I had to fight for my students, Devon and Kate. I know it seemed like I didn't trust you, and I am sorry for that."

"I appreciate that. I'll admit I'm not used to people taking a hand in the investigation the way you did, but I'm not sure I would have gotten it right without you bringing things to my attention."

"Thank you."

He stood up, and I stood up with him.

"This is your first year at the college, isn't it?" he asked.

I nodded.

"I hope this hasn't soured you on it. This can be a nice place to live."

"I'll keep that in mind."

Chapter 41

I had sent Mom and Dad a text Sunday morning, promising to call in the afternoon. After talking with Adams, I was glad I'd waited so I could give them all the facts.

After I laid it out for them, Mom said, "That was nice of the sheriff to come by and fill you in on the whole story."

"Let's remember," said Dad, "sheriffs are elected. He wants your vote."

"I know, Dad, but I think he was doing it to help me. He knows I went through a lot, and that this is my first semester here."

Dad went on. "That history professor is a monster."

"Yes, he is, Dad. And now he's in jail."

Mom asked, "Why would they let someone like that be a professor, let alone chairman of a department?"

"I don't think he was always like that. I'm sure for years he taught and did his research like the rest of us. I've read one of his books, and it's good. So he deserved to be on the faculty. But he's in his sixties now, and he said the biography he was writing would be the completion of his career. He couldn't stand the idea that Felix Fuchs and the commune he founded were in some ways on the wrong side of history. He didn't want that story to get out. Plus, it would reflect badly on his own ancestors."

"I see what your saying," said Mom, "but I don't like the idea of you living in a place like that."

"Mom, it's not 'a place like that.'" One man was

responsible for all this. He ordered the vandalism of my car to try to scare me away. He killed Kate Conrad rather than let her discover the truth. He spied on me, and, when he thought I was too close to the truth, he came after me.

"But now that man is locked up, and I think he will get convicted. He's not part of this place any more, and there are a lot of wonderful people here like Abbie and Lionel. Kate Conrad is gone, and she was a rare student, but I'll watch for another one to come along, and meanwhile I'll do my best for the others."

"Well, so long as you're safe."

We talked about what else was going on back home, and I told them how beautiful the fall colors were. They hadn't seen them since they'd made a trip to the East before I was born. I promised I would call again before the middle of the week.

Monday morning I felt free and easy about teaching and research—about everything, really. That quiet voice inside seemed to be asking, "What's the worst that could happen?" After all I'd been through, grumpy students, goofy colleagues, and gossipy staff didn't scare me. As I sat in my office at nine o'clock, enjoying the fall color, I laid out plans for that morning's art history class, content to give them something predictable and reassure them the exam would not be too difficult.

My phone rang, I answered, and a voice I didn't recognize said, "Good morning, Dr. Noonan. This is Georgina in President Taylor's office. How are you this morning?"

The candid reply would have been, "surprised to hear from the president of the college," but instead I said, "Fine, thanks. And you?"

"I'm just fine too. The president would like to speak with you and he has some time open in his schedule later this afternoon. Do you think you could drop by the office at three thirty?"

"I would be happy to."

"All right. We'll see you then."

We hung up, and I swiveled my chair to resume looking at the treetops. The yellow highlights were especially well lit this morning.

Maybe the president made a practice of inviting new faculty members to his office for a get-acquainted chat during their first semester, although, considering the events of the past week, maybe I was being called on the carpet for my part in getting Schumacher arrested. I would find out soon enough.

Art history went pretty much the way I had planned. Ursula Wilmot took her notes and seemed to be indexing them as she went. Byron Hawley struck his characteristic pose as the artist weighed down by petty concerns. The others politely responded when I posed questions to the class and otherwise distracted themselves with their cell phones.

My only problem that morning was two empty chairs. My eye kept darting to the places where I had last seen Kate and Devon sitting. I wondered if he would return for the remainder of the semester. I hated the idea that his education was being postponed by the unfair suspicion that had fallen on him, and I hated the thought that his family might blame him anyway. Kate would never return to a classroom and that made teaching just a job for me, a way to make a living.

There are worse ways.

After class I checked email and saw that the dean of students had written to all in the campus community re-stating the college's policy on inclusiveness: no discrimination based on race, religion, country of origin, or sexual orientation. I guessed this was in response to Friday's story in the student newspaper about Kate having a "lesbian affair." The dean's message wouldn't change anyone's attitudes or behavior, but I was glad to see it anyway.

The dean of faculty also had written to the campus community acknowledging news stories about the arrest of Professor Jacob Schumacher in connection with the murder of

Kate Conrad and promising full cooperation with the authorities. I had no doubt that Jacob was a killer, but I wondered if faculty, staff, and students who were "from around here" would choose instead to believe that the lesbian student and the outsider from San Francisco had robbed them of the college's grand old man.

I was distracted from these gloomy thoughts by a knock on my office door. There stood Devon, a shadow of his former self. No longer the action hero, he slouched, his head hung low. He looked pale, and I thought he might have lost weight.

"Can I talk to you?" he asked.

"Of course. Come in. Have a seat."

He perched on the edge of the chair, hands resting on his thighs. He kept his eyes down. His jaw worked as he decided where to start. "Teresa called me."

I waited.

"She told me she talked to the sheriff and told him I never hit her."

"I'm glad she did that."

He nodded. "She said her dad told her she could never talk to anyone about what happened that night, but she called the sheriff anyway to help me out."

"That's good."

"Yeah. I thanked her. She also told me you talked her into it. So, thanks."

"You're welcome. Are you glad to have that over with?"

"I guess, but it's all so screwed up. I didn't do anything wrong. She didn't do anything wrong. But we got separated, and I got a reputation as some kind of creep, and it was all so her dad could get elected."

So Abbie and I guessed right about that. "Are you going to see her again?"

"I don't know. It's been three years. We can't undo that."

"Three years might not be as long as you think."

"I guess."

"You've had a tough few weeks. We all have."

"Yeah. I just got back to campus last night. I've been home for the past week-and-a-half."

"How was that?"

He slid back in the chair and sat up straight. "Bad at first. Better since Teresa talked to the sheriff. Dad and I argued about whether I was coming back here. He kept telling me what I could and couldn't do, and how I was supposed to report to him. Then he said he was going to talk to campus security and see if they could keep me under a curfew. That's when I told him to forget it. I said I'd work, get an apartment, and go to community college. It just wasn't worth arguing with him any more. I'd rather do it on my own."

"But you're back."

"Yeah. After a couple days, he said I could come back to school here like before. I think mom talked to him."

"I'm glad it worked out. A lot happened while you were away."

He nodded. "I read the news about Dr. Schumacher. Why would a professor do that to a student?"

"People don't always want to hear the truth, especially not when it ruins the story they've been telling themselves. Schumacher's ideas about this place mattered more to him than the life of another human being."

He shook his head. "I also read the article in the student newspaper about Kate being gay. I feel bad for her. I guess I made it worse by asking her out."

"No you didn't. Everybody is just trying to figure out who they are and who they can love. That's not easy for anyone."

He looked out the window behind me for a moment, resting his eyes on the riot of color in the treetops. "I've been out of class for three weeks. I've already dropped two classes because there's no way I'll catch up in them. I wanted to see if I could make up the work in art history. I'll do all the reading, and I could do some library reports if that would help. I know it would be extra work for you, but if I could finish this course and two others, I could take a couple of classes over the summer and still graduate."

"I'll be glad to help you. Do the reading on the syllabus. Come by for my office hour on Wednesday, and we'll talk about it. Maybe next week you can make up a quiz and get back on track."

He took a deep breath and let it out. "Thanks, Dr. Noonan. I'll see you on Wednesday."

Chapter 42

When I walked into the outer office of the administration's suite, the lady at the desk looked up and said, "Good afternoon, Dr. Noonan." No five-second stare from her. "President Taylor is expecting you." She nodded toward the open door to an inner office.

When I appeared in the doorway, Taylor glanced up, smiled, and came around his desk to take my hand. He was very fit and perfectly groomed, but not as tall as he had seemed on stage when he addressed the faculty. "Dr. Noonan, thank you for coming over this afternoon. Please have a seat. Can we get you anything? Coffee? Water?"

"No, thank you."

We sat in a couple of armchairs by the window. I felt relieved that this was not going to be an across-the-desk conversation.

"Well," he began, perched on the front of his chair and leaning forward so he could speak softly, "Your first semester at Fuchs has been an unusually eventful one. I want to offer my condolences on the death of your student, Kate Conrad. I didn't know her personally. I'm sure that was shocking for you."

"Yes. She was quite a gifted student."

The president nodded his understanding. "Thank you for handling this the way you have. You've shown a lot of grace under pressure."

"You're welcome." Apparently, he hadn't heard about my

frantic barefoot run from the library to Abbie's Hutch on Friday afternoon.

He sat back and seemed to shift into a more expansive frame of mind. "You're aware the institution is changing. We're adding a school of business and becoming a university."

I nodded.

"We certainly have a lot of work to do, establishing the new school and building its reputation. At the same time, we want to build the quality and reputation of the School of Liberal Arts and Sciences. I hope everyone understands it would make no sense to declare ourselves a university and neglect the liberal arts."

Again, I smiled. "I'm happy to hear you say that."

"Good. I want to speak to you today because we also face a greater challenge. We have to make Fuchs—or whatever it is to be called—a different kind of institution, more cosmopolitan for one thing. I hope we can begin to recruit students from a wider area and even establish relationships with communities abroad. Our traditional base of students from southern Ohio will be better prepared for the economy of this century if they've learned to work with people from around the world."

"Sounds exciting," I said.

"Although I have almost no influence on hiring faculty, I have been pleased to see some recent hires from beyond our immediate area: yourself, of course, and for instance do you know Dr. Bell in the modern languages department?"

"Yes, we've met," I said with a straight face.

"Good. Other recently hired faculty have come from Atlanta, Houston, and Seattle. Also, to be perfectly candid, I think it's better for our students to see some persons of color among the faculty."

I smiled though I was going to be very disappointed if this was only a thanks-for-the-diversity conversation.

He continued. "Anything we can do to show our students that there's a wide world for them to explore. That's why I want to get your ideas about having an art gallery on campus."

I kept on smiling for a few seconds while my brain caught up with what he was saying. "That sounds exciting. What would be the purpose of this gallery?"

Now it was Taylor's turn to smile. "I think it could give our students a more cosmopolitan experience, expose them to creative trends in the world. Margaret and I were in Nashville last week, and at the university there they had an exhibit of paintings by contemporary African-American artists. They were amazing—such powerful images, vibrant colors. If we could do something like that here, it would give everyone on campus something to talk about."

My polite smile widened to a grin. "I agree. How can I help?"

"I'm hoping you would be interested in being the director of the gallery."

I searched my memory for a conversation with my fellow graduate students about what to say when they offer you your own gallery. Nope, that topic never came up. I resorted to honesty. "I don't know what to say."

He smiled. "Say you'll think about it. This is just the beginning of a conversation. I can think of a couple of rooms on campus that might be converted, but we would need your expertise there. I would need to know the budget for such an operation—something modest to begin with. Of course, we would reduce your teaching load so you would have time to do this, and I think an additional stipend would appropriate. There are a thousand details to work out. What I need today is to know whether you want to do it."

"President Taylor, there is nothing I would rather do than introduce our students to works of art."

"Excellent! I'm away next week, so let's talk again in about two weeks. Meanwhile jot down any ideas you have, any questions, and we'll start making this happen."

"Thank you," I said. "I suppose I should discuss this with my chairman, Frank Rossi."

"It was his idea."

I held my breath for a moment. "Really?"

"Yes. Apparently he told the dean we needed works of art on campus so you could teach art history. The two of them cooked up this idea of a gallery and brought it to the academic vice president, who mentioned it to me. Right away, I could see it would also do a lot for the whole campus. Even though it was Frank Rossi's idea, I wanted to talk to you personally to get the ball rolling."

Sensing we were done, I stood and walked to the door. He followed me and said to Georgina, "Let's set Dr. Noonan up for another conference when I get back from Atlanta."

She smiled. I smiled. He smiled and said, "Thanks again for dropping by."

I walked along the campus quad, not sure where I was going. I couldn't go back to my office, and work on quizzes, lessons, or even on my research. My mind was like a rock, rolling down a hillside, bouncing this way and that. I felt like getting in my car and driving around to see the fall color, but there were only a few hours of daylight left. Maybe Lionel would like to drive us and stop somewhere for dinner. I could knock on his door and ask.

When I got to College Avenue, instead of turning left toward Ohio Avenue, I turned right, went to the chapel, and let myself in. As I walked through the slanted rectangles of sunlight, I listened to the sound of my footsteps on the wooden floor. I faced the mural.

Six weeks ago, it had looked like a simple depiction of a community working and worshipping in its newfound Eden. A few weeks later, it had looked like a monument to a charismatic leader, Felix Fuchs. After further study, I had seen in it a record of people presuming to improve their species through selective breeding. And finally I had caught up to Kate's recognition of a symbol of evil, tucked away, up in the corner.

As I stood there, I couldn't see the image of the murdered child. The failing light left the top of the mural in darkness. But I would make sure the world saw it and knew that Kate Conrad had discovered it.

Thank you for reading *Dark Mural*.

If you enjoyed it, please help others find it by leaving a favorable review online.

Discover *Dark Exhibit*, Nicole Tang Noonan Mystery #2, at:
Dark Exhibit ebook on Amazon.
and visit:
http://www.RickHoman.com.

Made in the USA
Monee, IL
20 September 2019